THE TELLURIAN TERRORIST

Published in Canada by Engen Books, St. John's, NL.

ISBN-13: 978-1-77478-055-8

Distributed by:
Engen Books
www.engenbooks.com
submissions@engenbooks.com

First mass market paperback printing: July 2021

Cover Design: Ellen Curtis

Slipstreamers Committee:
Amanda Labonté
Ali House
AJ Ryan
Ellen Curtis
Erin Vance
Lauralana Dunne
Matthew LeDrew

THE TELLURIAN TERRORIST

LAURALANA DUNNE & JD RYOT

CHAPTER ONE

Cassidy stood tall in the cold, expansive hall. Head back and feet shoulder-width apart, she kept her spine straight as the tribunal filed back into the room.

It had been two days since the Tellurians had apprehended her. Two days since she had fallen through the wrong portal from Alluvia and ended up on the moon.

Cassidy grimaced. It was the first time she had ever encountered that particular phenomenon—multiple gateways in one location—and it hadn't helped that the rock system was identical between the three planets. She hadn't even known she wasn't on Earth until the Tellurian guards had picked her up walking down the dusty road. She realized something was amiss when they stopped their vehicle and got out to stare at her.

Humans and Tellurians didn't exactly share the same coloring. And while Cassidy's appearance seemed to be smack-dab in the middle of the two peoples—her hair too pale to be Tellurian, but her skin too vibrant to be Alluvian—her copper-colored hair was a dead giveaway.

The sound of a throat being cleared interrupted her thoughts and she snapped her gaze to the front of the room. She winced when she realized that this was not the first attempt to get her attention.

Five scowling faces were turned toward her.

"If you are ready, Ms. Cane?" the Tribunal Magistrate, an elderly woman with deep lilac-coloured skin and pale orange eyes, asked in a tone laced with irritation.

Cassidy ducked her head, feeling sheepish, and attempted to look remorseful. "Of course, Ma'am. I apologize."

The man sitting to the right of the woman sniffed critically. "Head Magistrate," he corrected, his salmon-coloured eyes hard.

This was not going well. Cassidy winced. "Apologies, Head Magistrate. I meant no disrespect." She reverently hoped that the Magistrates couldn't change their ruling mid-announcement. By the expressions on their faces, any favours that she may have won while presenting her defense had certainly disappeared.

"Ms. Cane," the Head Magistrate began, straightening in the centre chair. "You have been brought before us today on three different charges. We have heard your statement in response to your arrest. The two lesser charges are trespassing and theft. How do you plead?"

Cassidy cleared her throat. "Not guilty," she responded, feeling a twinge of accomplishment when her voice didn't waver.

One of the magistrates snorted and the Head Magistrate shot him a look. He stiffened with a scowl. She turned back to Cassidy. "Based on the ludicrous answers that you provided to our questions, this court has not only found you guilty of both charges, but we have also added the charge of contempt for making such a mockery of these proceedings. As for the higher charge: treason—"

"Wait, what?" Cassidy stepped forward. There had been no mention of treason at any point during the questioning. She knew nothing of the Tellurian's legal system—she had been operating blindly while trying to appeal to their sense of justice—but she had never heard of a situation where a treason charge was a good thing.

"We find you guilty," the Head Magistrate continued, as if Cassidy had never interrupted. The elderly woman stood and drew herself up to her full height. The other magistrates followed suit. A single shaft of light flickered to life and illuminated the area in front of her. "We will reconvene tomorrow after the median hour for sentencing."

The woman held her hands under the beam of light and clapped. The reverberations spread to the ends of the room, and Cassidy felt her bones rattle with the finality of the gesture. The beam switched off as the magistrates turned and shuffled from the room without so much as a backward glance toward her. Five heads of dark hair disappeared behind the closing door.

"Wait!" Cassidy called again. Rough hands grabbed her upper arms before she could take another step, and Cassidy was hauled backward. She struggled against the strong grip that held her, but it was to no avail. She was being pulled into the hallway.

Digging her heels into the door frame, she flexed her legs and was rewarded when the guard that held her grunted in surprise.

"There's been a mistake," Cassidy twisted her torso

to look up at his impassive face, but he just rolled his eyes and gave her petite form another tug. "I have to speak to them!"

With a snort, he dislodged her boots from the frame and dragged her from the room. The lightweight door zipped closed behind them with an upbeat chime, and Cassidy felt as though her only chance to reason her way out of this was cut off by the perky automated door.

CHAPTER TWO

Cassidy rubbed her hands together with more force than was necessary. Originally, when she had been returned to her holding cell, her heart had been pounding. That familiar excited feeling that she enjoyed—the tingling in her fingertips—had given her a high as she bounced around the small room, looking for a way to secure her escape. Hours later, alone and in the dark, she had finally given up her search.

She rubbed her hands together again to release her frustration before plopping down on the thin metal wall shelf that served as her cot.

The holding cell was unlike any that she had seen before, or been in… not that she had availed of many in the past. It was a singular room, but a force shield kept her confined to the back half of it—much like a specimen in a glass cage. Observers were free to enter the room from the large doorway that connected it to the hallway.

Observers, or interrogators.

Cassidy felt her stomach drop. She had spent several unsuccessful hours fiddling with the shield trying to figure out a way to stall its activation. Whenever she came too close to the metal lip on the floor, its sensor would pick up on her proximity and activate. There was nothing to do now but wait.

With a huff, she lay back on the cot. Morning would arrive soon. She would have to figure out a plan before her sentencing, otherwise her only option would be to try to escape during the transfer, and without knowing her way around that would be inconvenient at best.

Closing her eyes, Cassidy ran over everything she had learned in her short time on the moon. Maybe she would find some new information while sifting through her memories.

A soft click caught her attention. Cassidy held her breath as a harsh beam of light swept the holding cell, illuminating the backs of her eyelids as it passed over her. There was another soft click, and the room was plunged into darkness once more as the door swung shut.

The light had come from the hallway. Someone was in her room.

Forcing herself to breathe softly despite the pounding of her heart, Cassidy strained her ears for the slightest hint of a sound. The hum of the force shield generator was the only constant in the room, but she was positive that she could hear careful footsteps drawing closer to her cell.

Cassidy gave a soft murmur and stretched, rolling onto her side so that her back was against the wall. Her arm dangled over the edge of the cot so that her fingertips grazed against the cold smoothness of the floor. She cracked her eyes open into slits, hoping for all the world that whoever was in the room with her was under the assumption that she had only shifted in her sleep.

Her controlled breathing seemed too loud in her ears. Finally, after what felt like hours, the soft padding of quiet footsteps began again, and the slightest hint of a moving shadow came into view.

With painstaking slowness, Cassidy extended her hand until she felt the cool rim of her meal tray. The food remained, uneaten, where she had tucked it out of the way under her cot. At the top of the tray, however, was the battered metal fork that had come with it.

Cassidy stretched her fingers and secured the handle. It was a pathetic excuse for a weapon, but she would make it work if she had to.

A low chuckle gave her pause. "I wouldn't bother with that if I were you," the voice murmured. "Even with the force shield turned off, the sensors are programmed to pick up on anything that might be considered a weapon. You'll set off the alarm."

The voice was strangely familiar. Cassidy remained motionless; the fork clutched firmly in her fist as she opened her eyes.

The figure continued toward her and stopped a few feet before reaching the force shield. "Why else do you think they'd risk giving it to you?"

The voice remained soft as it spoke. It wasn't for her benefit to try and keep her calm, Cassidy decided. It was soft because it was trying to avoid detection.

Keeping a firm grip on the flimsy utensil, Cassidy swung to her feet in a fluid motion. Realizing that the intruder didn't want to be discovered shifted some of the power in the room to her favour. Regardless of their intent, Cassidy had the ability to alert the outside guards if necessary. The room was obviously not soundproof if they were whispering.

Cassidy took a step toward the barrier between them. "Who are you?" She kept her voice even but refused to lower it, feeling a twinge of satisfaction when her hunch was rewarded by the figure's flinch.

His face came into view as he stepped closer. Wide, intense yellow eyes fastened themselves on her face as he inspected her, much as she did him. His hair was dark, as was the case with most Tellurians, but his skin held a rusty-red tinge that she found fascinating.

"A friend," he said simply.

"I doubt it," she snorted. "Breaking into my room in the middle of the night doesn't seem very friendly."

He smirked and took another step closer, and Cassidy was able to place him. He was the Tellurian on the landing platform who had helped her to escape after she'd been discovered converting the irrigation system to allow for extra Chuga growth. "Who said anything about breaking in? What if I'm looking to break you out?"

He was offering her help for the second time. His answer stemmed the questions that Cassidy wanted to barrage him with. Instead, she crossed her arms over her chest and cocked her head. "I'm listening."

***

He remained motionless. Waiting. Assessing her.

Cassidy did the same. The silence stretched between them as they stared at each other over the marker of the unactivated force shield.

He unclipped a disc from his belt and held it in the

palm of his hand. Cassidy watched as it stretched and extended in a way that reminded her of a folding hand fan.
Her guest stared at it for a brief moment before taking a
step forward. She steeled her spine.

"How did you get to our moon?" His tone was carefully neutral.

Cassidy realized it was a test. "The Alluvian cargo
ship..."

He shook his head. "That was the first time. What
about the second time? If you had your own ship, you
wouldn't have returned here. You would have returned
home."

Cassidy frowned. If he knew her story, then he had
access to what she'd said in her defense hearing.

He sighed. "Your sentencing is tomorrow—"

"A portal," she blurted. She rubbed a palm against her
thigh in agitation. Cassidy hated telling anyone about the
portals. It was too big of a risk to let unknown alien races
know how to get to Earth.

Technically she wasn't revealing any information about
Earth. Just Alluvia, really. She calmed at the thought.

"I came here through a portal," she reiterated, squar-
ing her shoulders. There was no help for it. She had to get
out of here, now, and deal with this later. One problem at
a time, she told herself.

He gave an unsurprised nod and took a step forward.
"I want to hear all about it." He held her eye until she gave
a nod, agreeing to his terms. Satisfied, he tossed the disc
into the air between them. It sailed over the floor sensors
and hovered there as the shield activated—a bright wall
of light that shrank closer to the ground the lower that the

disc fell.

The disc rested on the sensors, reflecting the shield back into its source so that there was a gap in the wall.

"Hurry," he urged.

He didn't have to tell her twice. Cassidy dropped her fork with a clatter and slipped through the gap, turning sideways in order to fit through the small opening that the device created.

Once both feet were firmly planted outside of the holding cell, Cassidy turned to inspect the disc that disrupted the field that she had tried so hard to disable.

She had little time to assess it before a high-pitched whine reached her ears. She stared, dumbfounded, as the thin metal disc crumpled under her gaze, folding in on itself and disappearing as though it had never existed in the first place.

She gave a low whistle. "That's one way to cover your tracks."

The man next to her gave another low chuckle. "That's at least one of the things I pride myself on being good at."

Cassidy raised a brow and he dipped into a quick bow. "My name is Aldan, Cassidy Cane. And I have been looking everywhere for you."

CHAPTER THREE

Their escape from the government building went much more smoothly than Cassidy had expected. Aldan didn't use any technology to aid their flight. Instead, he wove them on a timed, backtracking path along the corridors that somehow let them avoid all of the guards that roamed the facility.

"There are others waiting for their hearings," he'd informed her as he eased open the door to her room, "so security is increased. Our best bet is to stay undetected for as long as possible so we can get out."

"And then?" Cassidy had asked, attempting to close her door behind them as noiselessly as possible.

Aldan had given a wry smile. "Run."

As luck—or Alden's training—would have it, they made it out without issue.

The chill of the outside hit Cassidy in the face as she sprinted down the manicured path after the Tellurian. She gulped down the night air, enjoying how fresh it felt in comparison to the recycled, temperature-controlled stuff she had been breathing for the past few days.

Aldan stopped without warning, and it was all she

could do to avoid colliding with him. He pivoted and grabbed her arm, giving it a tug as he dove behind the ornamental hedge lining the path. Cassidy followed after him.

They lay on their stomachs, panting, and attempted to catch their breaths. She turned to ask what they were doing, but Aldan raised a finger to his lips before she had the chance to speak.

She heard it then—the rumble of laughter accompanied by the sound of multiple footsteps. Several guards came up the hill, chatting among themselves as they made their way toward the building.

Shift change. Tellurians must have a heightened sense of hearing for Aldan to have picked up on their conversations from so far away.

Aldan raised himself up onto his elbows and watched them enter the building before letting out an exaggerated sigh. "That was close."

Cassidy cocked her head at him. "Was it? I feel like you've done this before a time or two."

"Once or twice," he grinned. Cassidy was struck by how the small expression lit up his face with mischief, making him appear youthful despite the gravity of the situation.

Cassidy couldn't help but grin in return. "Alright then. Since you're the expert: where to now?"

"Now? Now, we go. My craft is waiting."

Cassidy cast her eyes around, but all she could see was strange, flowering trees that dotted the rocky hills at random intervals. They reminded her of desert plants— large, spiked, weathered-looking things that jutted in all directions to fight for natural resources. They were nothing like the beautiful, delicate trees that grew in the Alluvian garden.

No grass grew anywhere in sight. The hedges and the trees were the only plant life next to them, and they only seemed to thrive due to the piles of the blue mulch heaped along their roots.

She raised her eyebrows in a question. There was no craft visible. The single point of entry into the complex was the stretching road that wove itself through a stone bridge and over a river that snaked through the property. There was no vehicle in sight.

"Craft?"

Aldan flopped onto the ground. "You didn't think we were going to walk, did you?" He winked and, before she could reply, stretched out and began to roll down the hill.

She watched, surprised, as he continued all the way to the bottom, stopping short of the rushing water and disappearing into the darkness of the shoreline's overgrowth— the only untended greenery around.

Cassidy waited for a telltale splash but heard nothing. Grumbling to herself, she followed suit and rolled into the darkness after him.

She came to a halt just before hitting the water. The thick, spiked plants that grew along the water's edge slowed her speed enough so that she could gain control of her descent.

Picking twigs out of her hair, Cassidy met the bemused gaze of Aldan. "Just a time or two?"

He grinned and gathered his feet beneath him. "Well,

maybe a time or four." He nodded ahead of them to the bridge. "We're almost there."

Cassidy rolled into a crouch and frowned. Not only was it the most unprotected spot in the whole complex, but it was also the most well-illuminated. Even the water plants around the bridge had been cut back to nothing.

"You want us to walk across the bridge," she asked in disbelief, careful to keep her voice low. "That's a terrible idea! The shift changeover is about to start."

Aldan waved his hand in dismissal. "Not walk. Fly."

When Cassidy blinked at him, he smirked. "Don't tell me that the Tellurian Terrorist is afraid of a little excitement."

Even in the dim lighting, Cassidy could see his pale eyes sparkle with the challenge, and she couldn't help but feel herself rise to it.

Her only response was a snort. Before he knew it, she launched herself forward and took off at a run, leaving him behind in her mad dash toward the bridge.

There was a muffled noise of surprise, and then the sound of even breathing as Aldan kept pace with her speed.

Cassidy resisted the urge to laugh. Despite herself, and the possible danger she was in, excitement was coursing through her veins and making her feel as though she were alive again.

A grumbling snagged her attention and Cassidy snapped her gaze to the quickly approaching road. A thick beam of light swept across the road as it rumbled toward the bridge.

"Get down!" Aldan hissed behind her.

Cassidy threw herself against the ground and was surprised to find that Aldan threw himself over her, covering her body with his own.

The light swept past them, and Cassidy jerked her head up in time to see a dilapidated vehicle, it's one lone headlight skimming across the road, sputter its way across the bridge and toward the building. She was able to distinguish the outlines of several passengers inside the vehicle.

If that's what stood for government technology on this planet, it was in worse shape than Cassidy had previously thought.

Several moments of tense silence passed. "You can get off of me now," she informed him, shifting her body to alleviate some of the weight on her pressure points.

"Sorry," he muttered. Instantly she felt lighter as shifted next to her. "My clothing blends into our surroundings better."

Cassidy couldn't fault him for that logic and dusted off her knees with a nod. "Now what?"

Aldan cocked his head and frowned. "You're right about the shift change. I can hear more vehicles on their way. More than usual. I wanted the distraction of the shift change to get you out, but I wasn't counting on the extra attention that tomorrow would bring."

"Extra attention?"

Aldan smirked. "It's not every day that you get to witness the sentencing of an off-worlder."

"Glad I could offer some distraction in these gloomy times," she quipped.

Aldan's smirk turned into a grin. He opened his mouth

to respond, but his expression faltered as more lights appeared in the distance.

Pulling up his sleeve, he tapped on a metal device around his wrist. A low-pitched whine filled the air around them. Cassidy took a step back when the surface of the river began to tremble.

She stood wide-eyed as water lapped furiously against the bank, cresting out in a convex shape by an unseen force above the river. The shape moved toward them from under the bridge.

Aldan tapped at his wrist again as there was a soft hiss. A porthole-sized opening rose outward, lifting mechanically out of thin air, and Cassidy could see the blinking lights of consoles floating in the space through it.

Aldan took one look at the approaching vehicles and stepped forward. He grabbed the rim of the opening and jumped through it. Cassidy was stunned to see him disappear, only to reappear a heartbeat later as he poked his head back through the opening. "Are you coming? The cover won't last for much longer!"

Cassidy gaped at him. He was sitting in a cloaked ship!

Her excitement was electrifying. Cassidy grabbed at the top of the opening and was shocked to find that she could grab the solid, cool material of the structure around it—even if she couldn't see it. Ignoring the lurch of her disconnected senses, she used both hands to lift herself up and swung herself through the opening after Alden...

—and landed right in a plush leather seat.

She tried not to let her jaw drop as her eyes roamed the inside of the craft. Blinking lights and controls were spread around her, taking up almost every space that the wall had to offer around the windows. Cassidy shook her head in disbelief. Everything inside the craft was invisible to the outside, but she had no trouble seeing the world around them.

"Buckle up," Aldan instructed, pressing a large button in the center console. The porthole cover hissed in response and began to close. He sat in the pilot's seat in front of her, settling into it as easily as she settled into her office chair at home. However, instead of grading student papers, he was tapping codes into the keypad in front of him to bring the machine around them to life.

The hatch clicked closed next to her, and Cassidy jumped as the locking mechanism's activation reverberated around them. She hastily buckled herself into her chair.

Mechanical lights stretched like glowing spider webs across the windows of the craft and Aldan swore under his breath.

"What's wrong?" Cassidy leaned forward and pressed her nose to the glass but could see nothing amiss outside around them.

"The cover is destabilizing."

"Meaning...?"

"Meaning we will be very visible, very shortly." He reached above himself and tapped finger on the glass over a gauge, as if telling it to hurry up. Cassidy watched the pointer tick up to the top level of the display with painstaking slowness. When it reached the top, an alert sounded, and Aldan breathed a sigh of relief.

"Finally," he muttered, settling back into his seat. His

fingers flew across the console, activating the engines and increasing their dull whine to a muted roar. "Cabin's pressurized. Hold on."

The craft jerked ahead with surprising speed. Cassidy clutched the flimsy arms of her chair as they shot down the river, the spray left in their wake slopping over the foliage and soaking the dusty shore.

Aldan pulled down on a large gear shift and the craft tipped back, the nose of the machine pointing up toward the lightening sky. The engines powered up and propelled them into the sky with a thunderous boom.

There was the sound of crumpling metal, and Cassidy watched as a piece of the craft detached and spiraled to the ground below. "Aldan…" Apparently all the machines on Telluria were in need of repair.

"It's fine. We got out of there just in time." He tapped the windshield, and Cassidy realized that the metallic glow had disappeared. "Our cover blew."

Cassidy peered out of the window. The craft's wings were visible, but there was no one around to see them. Clouds sped past them as they accelerated to dizzying heights. "Where are we going?"

Alden looked back at her and raised a brow. His coloring was more striking in the growing daylight—rusty red skin, dark hair, and daffodil-yellow eyes that mirrored the color of the clouds as they began to wake up for the day. Other than that, he looked like he could fit in at any cafe on earth. He looked positively human.

"We're going somewhere safe where we can talk. You promised to answer my questions, and once you do, I promise to take you home."

Cassidy tilted her head, noting that he had yet to level off their ascent. "And where, exactly, is that?"

Aldan tapped what looked to be coordinates into a map screen. When he caught her watching him, he rolled his eyes but didn't bother switching it off. They both knew she would never be able to recreate the journey.

"You'll see."

CHAPTER FOUR

They had been flying for what felt like hours. At no point did Aldan turn the aircraft any great degree or reduce their height. Instead, it was almost like he had enacted some type of cruise control that kept their heading and speed constant—something that would have worried Cassidy had he not been so attentive in their surroundings.

"Do you think we're being followed?" She asked at one point, noting how his attention kept shifting from the radar screen to the cloud-obstructed view around them.

"As a result of your break-out? No. I doubt it."

Cassidy felt her pulse pick up at his response. "But resulting from something else...?"

Aldan inclined his head, his eyes trained on the airspace around them. "Possibly. It depends on what the others have been up to."

Cassidy sat up straight in her chair. "Others?" When his only response was a shrugged shoulder, she crossed her arms. "You're leaving out a lot of information."

"That's something we have in common."

Cassidy settled back into her chair and said nothing.

The wind shifted and a mountain peak loomed in the distance. The rocky tip speared through the cloud cover, looking before them like a desolate beacon as Aldan maneuvered the craft toward it.

He grabbed a headband and positioned the attached yellow lens over one eye. To her surprise, he flicked off the navigation switches around him, powering everything down except for the engines.

Cassidy could feel a low rumble throughout her body. "What is that?"

"The volcano." He nodded toward the mountain peak.

It became louder the closer they came, and Cassidy could feel the thrumming in her ribcage despite being buckled securely in a pressurized cabin.

"The magma constantly churns inside of the mountain, circulating the molten rock. Whatever the rock is made of jams our electronic signals—"

"—making it the perfect place to hide," Cassidy finished. When Alden nodded, she frowned. "But what if the volcano blows its top?"

"That's when things get extra exciting."

Cassidy felt a twinge of annoyance at his cavalier attitude. "And what constitutes 'regular exciting?'" She'd been stuck inside a cramped aircraft for almost an entire day, unable to do anything but stare out a window and shift her weight in her seat. She was pretty sure her backside had become numb as a result. So far, her sentencing hearing would have been more interesting.

Aldan tapped a code into the console with a smirk. "This."

The engine output decreased immediately. There was a brief stutter of motion, then the craft began to fall. Cassidy refused to scream as she felt her stomach lurch up into her throat. Instead, she dug her fingers into the back of his chair in a death grip, her knuckles turning white.

Aldan laughed at her response and Cassidy couldn't help but stare. She had heard that laugh before. It was the type that was only born from testing yourself against impossible odds and emerging triumphant. It was a laugh of excitement and danger. It was a laugh that, so far, Cassidy had only ever heard come out of her own mouth.

Aldan expertly maneuvered the craft through the descent. The engine sputtered intermittently, providing a boost forward during their fall that confused Cassidy until she noticed that each sputter corresponded with a flash of light on the lens he wore.

He was hitting invisible checkpoints on their route. Wherever they were headed, and whoever was there waiting for them, must have some of the most advanced security features that Cassidy had ever encountered. She fervently hoped that his cocky attitude was well-earned. She had no desire to see how the security system reacted if they didn't correctly identify themselves.

The engines kicked back in and slowed their descent. Aldan gave a self-satisfied hum and lowered the craft, skimming the tree line close enough that the highest branches swayed with annoyance.

Cassidy wondered if she would have a chance to explore planet-side before returning home. She had never seen trees like this before—they were nothing like the ones that grew outside of the Tellurian government building.

They reminded her of stinger nettles back on Earth. Long branches stretched out of thin spiny trunks toward the sky, but the needles that adorned the deep green leaves looked like claws grasping at the weak sunlight that was filtered by the thick cloud cover. The closer they came, the more easily she could make out large swaths of browned and crumbling vegetation.

"The added cloud coverage from the volcano must make it hard to get around. You're a very good pilot."

When Aldan blinked at her in confusion she clarified. "Back home we have instruments to help us navigate around volcanoes. The additional smoke plumes can be hard to see through."

Aldan shook his head. "We have the technology to navigate through clouds as well. We have to. But this volcano has no plume. That's why it blocks signals so well. Everything is contained within the mountain."

Cassidy eyed the tree line again. "Then why is it so hard for the sunlight to pierce the clouds? The plants are dying."

"Plants are dying all over Telluria." His voice was carefully neutral when he responded, but Cassidy could hear the tinge of control waver when he spoke. "This cloud system stretches across the entire moon. That's why the growing stations you visited are so important for our survival."

His careful words were like a punch to the gut. Her sinking feeling had nothing to do with Aldan landing the craft, and everything to do with the guilt that was blooming in her chest.

Aldan hovered over a small landing strip before

touching down with a thump, depressurizing the cabin and then opening the porthole with the click of a dial.

He swung himself from the hatch with ease and turned to see if she needed any assistance.

Cassidy accepted it and bit back a groan as she balanced on her cramped legs, stretching them once she was back on solid ground.

The area around them was dark and damp. There was no sign of any plant or animal life running through the mud, unlike in the swamps or bogs back on Earth. Here it was impossible for anything to grow underneath the tree canopy.

Aldan gestured ahead of them. At the edge of the landing strip stood a derelict shed—a refueling station was her best guess—the only structure that Cassidy could see around them.

"Cassidy Cane," Aldan's voice seemed thin in the empty air around them, "welcome to the home of the Tellurian Resistance!"

CHAPTER FIVE

The little shack was lackluster at best. At first Cassidy thought that the tiny building was a joke, and she wondered what she had managed to get herself into by agreeing to the break-out with Aldan. Then, to her immense relief, he'd pushed aside the heavy-looking storage crates with a touch of his wristband.

The metal floor paneling slid across the room and created an opening large enough to display a locked hatch under the floor. Leaning forward, he punched a code into an unlit keypad and was rewarded with a beep from the locking mechanism as the hatch popped open.

"Your security measures are very extensive," she told him as he gestured for her to take the lead into the depths below.

"They have to be. We can't leave anything to chance."

Cassidy grasped the smooth metal rungs of the ladder and let the darkness swallow her. "And your aircraft?"

"Already hidden. The landing platform retracts underground." Aldan flexed his fingers. Cassidy heard a clicking sound, and bright beams of light shot out from the tips of his glove.

Aldan followed after her, locking the entryway above them with ease. He jiggled the handle to make sure that it had closed. She heard the metal floor slide back across the hatch as he joined her in her descent.

Cassidy reached the bottom and eyed the glove with interest. "I've got to get me one of those," she murmured.

Aldan grinned, locating a hidden marker that Cassidy couldn't see and trudging toward it. "I'm sure we have an extra one lying sound somewhere that could find its way into your pocket," he replied, motioning for her to follow him.

She looked around, unable to differentiate between the labyrinth of tunnels that branched out from where they stood, then followed him with a shrug.

The only sound was the shallow scuffing of their footfalls against the packed earth under their boots. The sound of the pinging of the metal pipes disappeared behind them as they went deeper underground.

Aldan swept his hand ahead of them, the lights in his gloves outlining the dark interior of the tunnels and the different paths that stretched endlessly before them. "These were once mining tunnels," he told her, stepping unerringly in a direction with a conviction that left Cassidy baffled. "The mines were abandoned once the volcano became more active. The churning of the core disrupted the mining instruments too severely to be of any use. Wherever melted minerals were dredged up from the inside of the moon didn't agree with the Sublunaries's technology and caused the robots to keep deactivating. So they abandoned the project."

Cassidy noted that his disdain for the Alluvians was a

near-match to how the Alluvians felt about the Tellurians. "Plus the volcano could erupt at any time... right?" Cassidy found that the hum of molten activity was growing louder the deeper they went into the tunnels. She wouldn't want to be trapped here if it decided to blow its top.

Aldan quirked a sardonic half-smile. "Right," he said, but his tone implied that that was never a factor in the decision. He pivoted so abruptly that Cassidy would have collided with him if she hadn't been paying attention. He peered at the opening of a new corridor, then gave a satisfied nod before leading them down it.

Cassidy could see nothing marking the way. "How do you know where to go? Forgive my skepticism, but it seems unlikely that you have the path memorized..." Her voice trailed off in a drawl as a rockslide loomed ahead of them, cutting off their route.

Aldan took a step forward. "I can't tell you all of our secrets, Cassidy Cane," he murmured.

To her immense surprise, he reached out and pressed random rocks in the pile of rubble. There was a change of pitch in the hum around them. He threw a smirk over his shoulder and stepped forward, leaving her gaping as he walked through the rocks and disappeared in front of her.

"You better be dreaming, Cassidy," she muttered to herself, hurrying after him in an attempt to keep up. She held her arms in front of her, expecting the resistance of the stones, but she felt nothing as she walked right through the rock pile. A well-lit tunnel stretched before her on the other side. It was almost like walking through a portal.

Aldan shot her a bemused look. "The light projection remains intact. I just shut off the force shield."

Cassidy schooled her expression. "There never was a cave-in in the tunnel."

"There never was a cave-in in the tunnel," he confirmed her statement, motioning to a large, locked door ahead of them. He took off his glove and held his hand against a lit pad. There was a beep when the scan completed, and a click as the door unlocked at his touch. He swung it open with a dramatic flair and gestured for her to take the lead.

Cautiously, Cassidy stuck her head through the exit and was greeted by the sight of an empty, windowed dome. She stepped forward and, waiting as Aldan secured the door behind them, peered out through the glass before them.

The glass entrance dome was situated above a large room. It jutted out from the top, much like a bay window would on a house, and allowed Cassidy an unobstructed view of everything below her — as well as an unobstructed view of her to everything below her.

Several heads craned upward and stared at her with surprise. Others looked at the string of alarms that stretched across the walls, as if waiting for a sign that they had to spring to action at her presence. The alarm system remained dark and quiet, offering no explanation.

Aldan took up the position next to her. The people below them visibly relaxed, and a wave of tension left the room at the sight of him.

Aldan removed his headband, powering down the lens — the thing that had undoubtedly allowed him to see the hidden markings in the tunnels, and tucked it under his arm. "Cassidy Cane, the Terrorist of Telluria, welcome to the true home of the Tellurian Resistance."

CHAPTER SIX

Cassidy paced the hallway in agitation. It had been over an hour since Aldan had entered the meeting chamber and she hadn't heard a sound since. She had caught sight of three official-looking Tellurians waiting in the room, scowling at him, before the door was unceremoniously closed in her face. No one had checked on her since.

She ran her hands through her hair, feeling the snarls and tangles that had accumulated from her adventures over the past few days. She used her fingers to comb it out in an attempt to look more presentable, using the hair tie around her wrist to secure her fiery stands when she was finished.

What she wouldn't give to have a shower.

This area of the underground compound seemed newer than the rest. Cassidy found her attention trailing along the walls to where the adjoining concrete tunnels connected at different intervals of the hallway.

"No one said I couldn't explore," she murmured to herself. Tellurian technology continued to surprise her. If she could have some time to herself to analyze it uninterrupted...

The large door opened with an audible strike against the latch plate. An older gentleman stuck his head around the doorframe. Curious lilac eyes met her own. "Cassidy Cane? Please come in." he opened the door in polite invitation.

She offered him a smile. "Thank you," she murmured, inclining her head as she stepped past him into the room...

—and came to an immediate halt when she realized that it looked almost identical to the courtroom where she had tried pleading her case only yesterday.

Cassidy tried not to feel anxious as the door was closed and locked behind her.

***

"Cassidy Cane," a soft voice greeted her with surprising warmth.

Cassidy's uneasy sense of deja-vu continued as an elderly woman stepped ahead of the small crowd that had assembled for the meeting. She had the same lavender skin as the Head Magistrate, but her demeanour was softer as her yellow eyes appraised Cassidy with interest.

"My sister was right to alert us to your presence."

Cassidy blinked. "Sister?" She looked to Aldan for confirmation, but he only raised an eyebrow in response. Of course, they would have to have someone on the inside, Cassidy realized. How else would he have known where she was being held?

"I am Taleia," she introduced herself. "Please," she took a step back and gestured to the table and chairs next to her, "take a seat. We have much to discuss."

Cassidy raised her eyebrows but accepted the invitation. She was pleased when, after everyone else took their positions around the meeting table, someone bustled in from a side door with trays of food and drink. Realizing how dry her throat had become, she snagged a glass of water as they were being passed around.

Cassidy almost choked when the bitter liquid hit her throat. While it helped to slake her thirst, it was nothing like the flavour she was expecting. She noticed that everyone around her drank without complaint and wondered if someone had slipped something into her glass.

Small baked loaves were passed around next, and Cassidy's stomach grumbled in response. She took a hesitant bite of the blue-tinged pastry but chewed quickly once the flavour of milled flour hit her tongue. The others dunked their bread in their cups and Cassidy followed suit, noting in surprise that the loaf tempered the strange flavour of the liquid.

"I've read your file," Taleia continued, content to fill the room with speech while the others looked on, "so I understand what your mission was once you came to Telluria… but what I'm interested in is the 'why.'"

Cassidy finished her loaf and wiped her fingers in her pants. "Why what?"

Taleia leaned forward, eyeing Cassidy earnestly. "Why did you conspire with the Sublunaries to sabotage our crops? You seem like a highly educated woman—the opposite of how our government's smear campaign describes you," Cassidy raised her brows at that, but Taleia continued, "so why attack us without provocation?"

Cassidy leaned back, away from Taleia's scrutiny, and took stock of the room around her. Everyone at the table, Aldan included, had given her their undivided attention. Mistrust simmered in some of their pale gazes, some were tinged with anger as they waited for her reply, but despite the unpleasantness of the emotions that hung in the room, no hostility painted the faces that were turned toward her. Just open-minded curiosity.

They were nothing like the Alluvians had led her to believe, and not for the first time since coming to Telluria did Cassidy feel a sinking in her stomach.

She cleared her throat. "I assume by "Sublunaries," you mean the inhabitants of the planet that you orbit?"

Taleia gave a stiff nod. "That is what we call them, yes. You might know them as Alluvian."

Cassidy cocked her head, her mind moving too quickly to realize that her mouth was about to get her into trouble. "But you call them Sublunary? Because they are *sub-par* in relation to Tellurians?"

Taleia's brows shot toward her hairline, but the male sitting next to her interjected before she could. "Because their needs are not more important than the Tellurian's," his voice was a practiced mild rebuke, but his gaze slid to Aldan, as if blaming him for Cassidy's outburst.

Aldan's face colored uncomfortably under the attention of the older gentleman, and he slid down a little in his chair.

"But they are the ones who provide you with food."

"We provide them with food!" The man retorted, his fist banging the table in emphasis loud enough to make everyone jump. "And because of it we are stuck, beholden to them as their greed grows. They withhold technology from us and dictate how we are to live all so that they are able to grow fat on our labour while our own children starve—"

"Their children are starving," Cassidy interjected, her voice low enough to cut through his speech. "They give you the means to feed yourselves and yet you withhold food—"

"Withhold food!" Matching her intensity, the man rose and leaned toward her over the table. "We have done no such thing."

"I've seen the silos—"

"Did you go *in* them?" he sneered. "Did you see how little we've been able to put aside for emergencies? How close we are to starvation? Those silos house the entire moon's food supply!"

Cassidy stared at him, dumbfounded. He was right. Cassidy hadn't even checked on their supply level. She hadn't bothered to validate the Alluvians's story. She had been so preoccupied with saving their children and securing their lung-scanning technology, that she hadn't seen their story for the lie it was. That was before she'd learned that the Alluvians had planned to blow her up instead of coming to her aid, of course. Before Aldan had stepped in and saved her.

Taleia raised her palms to halt the conversation. "That is quite enough, Mycah," she admonished, her voice soft. "Cassidy is our guest and unfamiliar with our customs, and what actually happens on Telluria. Yelling at her will not teach her any faster, nor will it warm her to our cause."

The man, Mycah, had the grace to look abashed and seated himself without another sound.

Cassidy crossed her arms. She watched Mycah, unconvinced, but when his full attention remained focused on Taleia, Cassidy slid her gaze to the woman instead. "And what is your cause, exactly?"

Taleia sat back in her chair. She placed tapered fingertips to her left temple and began to rub it slowly, looking very tired all of a sudden. "What did the Alluvians say to you to convince you to commit your act of sabotage?"

Cassidy weighed her options for her response. Initially she had told the Tellurian Government that she had flown her own vessel to the moon as an independent act of defiance, but with the admission of portals to Aldan earlier...

She looked over and saw that he was the only other person in the room watching her, his yellow eyes unreadable as he waited for her response. Their eyes met and he cocked his head and raised a brow. *Go on*, his expression told her.

She realized there was no help for it. They'd find out eventually. The Tellurian Government was probably already combing the area where they found her. They may have already located the portal system. For all she knew, they were having tea with Gamgee at this very moment.

Cassidy raised a brow back at Aldan and returned her attention to Taleia. "I'll tell you everything you need to know, but first you must do something for me."

Taleia's brows flattened, and Cassidy fought the need to wince. "I don't mean to sound ungrateful," she continued, her voice softer. She had to be careful. She wanted them sympathetic, not offended.

Cassidy cleared her throat. "I really appreciate you getting me out of that cell. Aldan took no small risk, and I am grateful to him for that—but this isn't about me. I have family and friends to think about—a whole planet to protect. I need assurances."

A murmur went through the room at her statement. Taleia sat up straight in her chair at Cassidy's proclamation. "And which planet is that, Cassidy Cane?"

Cassidy placed her hands in her lap to steady herself. She felt an unexpected lump form in her throat at the thought of Earth—her parents and her siblings, and yes, even of Gamgee, who must be wondering where she was as her fake Cancun holiday was past its end.

Home...

She cleared her throat. "A planet far away," she said softly, to the curious faces that had turned toward her, "that is unaware of my ignorant trespassing, and of any damage that I may have done. It is innocent, and it deserves to be kept out of whatever ongoing conflict between your two worlds that I seem to have inadvertently put myself in the middle of, and I intend to make sure it remains safe."

"And what do you require to do that?" Taleia probed in the growing silence after Cassidy's impromptu speech.

"Explosives," Cassidy responded without hesitation. Taleia pressed her lips together, and she raised a hand to stem the woman's silent disapproval. "Not weapons— though yours do seem to be much more advanced than anything we have back home. But that's exactly why I need them to stay here. I want an explosive big enough to ensure that once I'm through the portal no one will follow after me. I want to seal it shut."

The murmuring began in earnest when she finished, and Cassidy let them argue among themselves. She didn't have to persuade anyone—she knew she had the upper hand. They needed her more than she needed them. She wanted to get back to Earth as soon as possible, but not if it meant risking the planet. Not if it meant risking her friends. Both the Alluvian and Tellurian technology was far more advanced than anything available on Earth—she couldn't let it follow her back. Spending the rest of her life as a guest of the Tellurian Resistance was the better option, and she knew that they knew she was right.

Her attention turned to Aldan. He remained quiet during the debate that raged around them. His self-satisfied smirk shone like a beacon in the room, and Cassidy wondered how much of her rescue had been his idea, or if he had even had the blessing of the Resistance. Judging by his cat-that-ate-the-canary expression, she had no trouble believing that he had assigned himself a solo mission.

He knew that portals—or something like them—existed. She had been nothing but the pawn in a long-standing game between the two planets that happened to arrive with the proof. Lucky her.

Taleia also noticed Aldan's expression and frowned. She placed her palms on the table. It was an understated move that generated no noise, yet the entirety of the table fell silent with the small gesture. All eyes turned to the woman seated at the head of the table, and Cassidy couldn't help but feel impressed at the quiet power that the woman held over the group.

Taleia met Aldan's gaze until he began to fidget under her attention. "We will speak about this later," she informed him. "Privately."

Aldan had the grace to look abashed. "Yes, Grandmother."

Cassidy didn't have time to react. Taleia's yellow gaze slid to her, commanding Cassidy's full attention. The two women stared at each other, silent, until Taleia returned her fingers to her forehead with a sigh. "Portals," she muttered to herself, almost inaudibly, resuming the circular rubbing against her temple as the room held its breath.

"The Council has heard your request, Cassidy Cane. And while we will debate the merits of the situation later, I want the whole story from the beginning. All of it. Leave nothing out. We will then evaluate our next moves accordingly."

Taleia straightened her spine and waited for any rebuttal, but no one interjected. The Council was letting her run with it, and for that Cassidy was unsure if she was grateful or apprehensive.

"You've made a fine mess for Telluria, Cassidy Cane. Now it's time for us to figure out how to best clean it up."

Cassidy felt her stomach drop. Apprehensive... Definitely apprehensive.

Taleia lifted the large pitcher of water and poured a generous glass, sliding it to Cassidy. She smirked, but not unkindly. "Now, if you please. From the beginning."

CHAPTER SEVEN

Cassidy took another sip of the tepid water, rolling the unfamiliar flavour over her tongue. There were minerals in it she couldn't identify—not surprising, since she was on a different planet—and while it didn't taste *bad*, it certainly didn't quench her thirst like she was used to. It wasn't as crisp as the water she was used to drinking on Earth. None of the others seemed to have the same feelings about it as she did, so she said nothing. There was much that she didn't know about Telluria, and so far, she was only beginning to scratch the surface of it.

They had gone over everything twice now. The first time she had told the story without interruption. She had only briefly touched on the backstory of her exploring different worlds through the portals with Gamgee—she had left him completely out of it—and let them think that it was of her own accord that she was here. The last thing she needed was to incite a panic that Earth's government would storm through the moon looking for her if she didn't return on time. Glossing over unnecessary Earth information, she began the story in earnest when she arrived on Alluvia. She described the desert-like conditions that she encountered outside of the cave-system. After all of the archaeological digs that she had taken part in in her lifetime, Cassidy was no stranger to surviving in deserts, but the rapt expressions of those around her reminded her of the wonder that she had first experienced when face-to-face with a terrain of sand and sky and a harsh sun beating down on her.

"I've heard the Alluvians describe their planet before, but I never truly believed what they were saying," one of the councilmen had said in a hushed tone. The others around him shushed him into silence.

That was the only interruption the first time through. Unsurprisingly, they made her tell it again. This time, they interrupted her to ask questions, clarifying different parts of her story and taking notes. She was unsure if it was for their own information, or if it was a test on the validity of her story, but eventually they seemed satisfied and had stopped asking questions. Most had excused themselves and rushed from the council chambers without a backward glance.

Cassidy sipped her water again, enjoying the rest no matter how brief. She became acutely aware that she had not slept in some time and could feel the exhaustion tugging at the corners of her senses as she fought to remain alert in her chair.

Aldan remained. As did Taleia.

"If what you say is true," Taleia began, holding up a hand to deflect any offense that her words may have caused but Cassidy just shrugged, she was too tired to be offended at this point, "then the Alluvians are in a much worse position than we are."

Aldan cocked his head. He folded his legs under him in the chair and leaned forward. "How so? They are not the ones trapped on their planet."

"They are, but for different reasons," his grandmother disagreed with a shake of her head. "And they are stuck not being able to use their planet. We always thought that the scattered visitor wore their breathing equipment on Telluria because of our atmosphere, but if what Cassidy says is true..." Cassidy waved her hand to show that she again took no offense with Taleia's doubt, "they are only capable of surviving in their domes without them."

Aldan slapped the table in front of him in exasperation, causing Cassidy to twitch in her tired state. "That doesn't excuse them ruining our food supply and endangering Tellurian lives!"

He hushed his tone part way through with a look from Taleia, and she pressed her lips together in thought. "No, it certainly does not."

"Why can't the Alluvians grow their own food?" Cassidy asked, draining her glass of the remaining water. "Wouldn't it be easier for them to set up their own growing stations instead of shipping the fertilizer up here to use in yours?"

Aldan snorted and Taleia shook her head. "It's not a fertilizer—though I assume the properties are similar. It's a growing agent. It's synthetic enzymes that transform the soil to make it more receptive to the crops we sow so that it's possible to grow them."

Cassidy blinked in surprise. It made sense. If the outside vegetation—or lack thereof, depending on what part of the planet she was located on—was any indication of the growing environment, nothing here would be edible for humanoids. "That's amazing!"

Taleia dipped her head in a nod.

"The Alluvians destroyed their planet—the soil, the water —the very air they breathe is poison. It's impossible to grow anything in that environment," Aldan expanded with a shrug. "They don't have enough resources to use space in their domes."

"So it's easier to set up proper lighting and ship this chemical agent here as opposed to shipping everything the planet would need to grow their own supplies," Cassidy murmured. She thought back to the transport ship she had used and had to agree. The sheer volume of water and soil that would constantly have to be harvested from the moon seemed like an impossible task for the tiny ship. The Alluvians already treated their own drinking water, but the amount that would be needed to grow their own food would be impossible.

"Easier, but not easy." Taleia sighed. "The ground needs pre-treating. Lights need to be created—no doubt you've noticed our cloudy atmosphere—irrigation systems need to be created and installed... It's doable with help from the Alluvian government, but it can take years just to get the supplies here. Chuga takes a massive amount of resources to grow."

"They don't have that kind of time."

When the Tellurians blinked at her, Cassidy cleared her throat. "I've seen their medical scans... I think they need more Chuga because their deficiencies are getting worse. Their children's survival is in danger. Now. Some of them may not last the current growing season."

The last part came out in a whisper, and both Taleia and Aldan's expressions became grave.

"But why ship the growing agent? Why not just get you to create it here?" Cassidy knew that pollution was a concern for the planet, so why would they knowingly contribute to it when they could just as easily create it on Telluria? Even on Earth, the pollution created by synthetic fertilizers was concerning. She could only imagine that creating something that essentially rewrote the nutritional compounds of the soil itself must also be high on that list.

Aldan snorted, his face an expression of disdain. "They won't tell us how to make it."

Cassidy blinked at him.

She looked at Taleia who gave a quick nod. "They worry that if Tellurians knew how to create the agent, we would then look for compensation for the food—an arrangement they are willing to avoid at all costs."

Cassidy frowned. "And if you can't make it—"

"—Then we have no control over our own food supply." Aldan finished. "They want to keep us fully dependent upon them. Even the knowledge of space travel is guarded with jealousy. Only their robots function as mechanics should something go wrong during a transport run."

Cassidy frowned and tapped her fingers on the table. It was the only sound in the vast room before she stilled. "I'm sorry," she told them, her shoulders slumping, "for the part I played, as ignorant as I was about it. Your people are in danger and it's all my fault."

The silence grew between them until Taleia spoke.

"Then make it right," she told her, her voice soft. "Fix the mistake that you made."

Cassidy stretched out her hands. "How?"

"Take us to your portal. Lead our team onto the Alluvial home world so that we may replenish what was destroyed." Taleia reached out to take Cassidy's hands in her own. "Lead our people to freedom, Cassidy Cane. We can't do it without you."

CHAPTER EIGHT

Aldan led the way through a set of double doors. The smell of cooking food wafted toward them, causing Cassidy's stomach to growl in response. She couldn't remember the last time she had eaten a full meal.

She trailed him into the mess hall and stood next to him in the service queue, noting how the room resembled any of the dozens of cafeterias that she had been in on Earth.

"Tell me about the Alluvian facility," Aldan probed, scanning the room with a thoughtful expression on his face.

Cassidy followed his gaze and was unsurprised to find that most of the attention in the room was fixated on her. Some averted their eyes, but others stared openly at her, meeting her gaze in a way that made her grateful for Aldan's company in the large room. Their expressions hovered between curiosity and hostility, and Cassidy decided that she didn't want to give them the chance to explore either.

"*Terrorist,*" she heard someone hiss behind her, and she twisted to see a small group of diners exit the room.

Aldan watched her; his brows raised as he waited for her response. Cassidy pulled her attention back to their conversation as best she could. "Similar to this, actually."

Aldan's expression turned to disbelief, so she continued.

"I mean, the technology is more advanced, yes. But the basic structure is similar. The major difference is that their buildings are above ground. They are also air-tight where they rise above the dome."

Aldan snorted as they moved up in the line. Cassidy noticed that no one joined it behind them. "They have no choice but to keep out the air," Aldan growled, his posture becoming tense. "Their air is poison. *They* are poison. And now they seek to spread that poison to Telluria? I will not allow it."

Cassidy pursed her lips at his bravado. "What they did—what they tricked me into doing—was despicable, yes. But I don't think greed or hatred was the motivator. I think it was fear." Aldan slid his gaze toward her, so she continued. "Their population is still growing. They're at a standstill with what they can do on Alluvia, but they're unable to leave. Physiologically, they can't survive in your atmosphere any easier than they can in theirs. They need resources and they need them now."

"That's no excuse to endanger us," Aldan shot back, stepping forward with such force that his boot stomped on the floor before he could control himself.

"You're right," Cassidy agreed. Those closest to them were casting hard looks in her direction. "There's no excuse for that. But sometimes, I think, when you have to choose between the certain hardship of your loved ones and a potential one for those you have never met, everyone tends to embrace the former rather than the latter. It's definitely not a situation I envy them being in."

Aldan's posture relaxed and he looked at her with interest.

Cassidy took the opportunity to ask a question that was bugging her. "Why destroy your supplies, though? Surely you would just replace them?"

"We can't eat the chuga. It's poison to us. Our bodies have adapted to needing less vitamin D because of our atmosphere, so we are unable to filter out the extra vitamins and our organs shut down. I suspect the plan was to leverage our agent as payment for the extra Chuga, while negotiating for more fields at the expense of our own growing space."

"Oh."

The line moved forward and Aldan was next for the servers. He pressed a code into the keypad which hummed in response. There was a soft churning, the sound of mechanized wheels behind the scenes, then everything halted with a cheery *ding!* that caused Cassidy to stifle a grin. A thin metal door rolled up and two serving trays slid forward onto the small shelf.

Aldan handed the first one to Cassidy before taking his own and leading the way to a pair of vacant chairs.

Cassidy set her metal tray on the cafeteria table and immediately heard the scraping of chairs around her. She watched as some of the Tellurians closest to her abandoned their meals to exit the mess, muttering between themselves.

Cassidy swung herself into her seat and sniffed at her

clothing. "Do they find my smell offensive?"

Aldan sat across from her and took a long drink of water before answering. "I think it's your 'Tellurian Terrorist' title that they find offensive, if anything."

Cassidy winced, and he shot her a sympathetic look before tucking into his food. She picked up a pronged utensil and attempted to do the same.

Almost everything on the tray was tinged with blue. Several types of oddly-shaped vegetables—something that she would have called prehistoric carrots if she were back on Earth—were nestled in the pockets of the dish. Long thin grains, reminiscent of rice, filled a bowl and smelled faintly of salt and herbs. Even the tea had a blue tinge to it.

The only thing spared from the color was the bland-looking white fish that still rested on its skewers. Without hesitation, Cassidy began to unceremoniously shove the grilled fish into her mouth.

"It must be hard to sustain wildlife on your moon," she said after eating half of it, breaking the silence.

Aldan pursed his lips, spoon hovering in the air with his next bite of food. He cocked his head as if he had never considered it. "Yes, and no," he replied after a moment's thought. "Fish are easy. Low-light plants grow in our waters, which allow support for them as well as insects. The larger meat sources are much more complicated."

"Such as the vecas?"

Aldan nodded. "The Alluvians have found a way to supplement and synthesize the vecas's food supply within their enclosures, allowing them to graze. It is not something that we grow here."

Cassidy chewed her fish. That made sense. It was easier to allot space and resources for grass in comparison to an entire population's food supply.

"Are there any natural predators?"

"Not on land." When she raised her eyebrows, he grinned. "We get the odd fisher's tale, for sure. And sometimes larger beasts wash up on shore. But so far, no one's ever been able to catch one."

Cassidy nodded and popped a shriveled root vegetable into her mouth. "It took us a very long time on Earth before we were able to capture large sea creatures."

Aldan's yellow eyes became curious. "You'll have to take me some time."

"To Earth?"

"Yes…. Tell me about it?"

Cassidy tilted her head. "A question for a question," she offered, taking a sip of her drink.

Aldan paused his eating at her serious expression. "Very well," he agreed, solemnly.

Cassidy cleared her throat. "Why did you help me?" When he looked surprised, she clarified. "After I sabotaged the irrigation system. You knew what I had done, and yet you helped me to escape. Why?"

Aldan gave a shrug. It was meant to come off as impish, but he didn't quite hit the mark. "We'd intercepted a communication from the Alluvian government warning us of an alien ship in orbit around their planet. It piqued my interest." When Cassidy blinked in surprise he continued. "They don't know how much our sensors have advanced in the past few years. I knew that there was no ship in orbit. Just as I knew there was no ship present when you were arrested upon your return." Realization clanged through Cassidy. No wonder he had been watching for her return—he had already had suspicions about the portals. "And I knew a transport vessel was arriving when we received the warning. The timing was too coincidental. I assumed they were setting up a scapegoat. And I know all too well what the government does to criminals."

His voice was low with the last sentence. Cassidy felt her mouth go dry and took a sip of her drink to try and ease it. She had already contaminated the irrigation system when Aldan had caught up with her, and even knowing what she had done he had saved her anyway.

Cassidy swallowed. "Thank you." Her voice came out hoarse despite her best efforts. It was too simple a thing to say to someone who had done so much for her.

Aldan shrugged off her thanks. "I should be thanking you."

"Thanking me?"

Aldan smirked and leaned forward. "I love it when my interest is piqued."

Cassidy felt her cheeks redden under the weight of his stare. She used the pronged utensil to shove another piece of the crispy fish into her mouth. "What would you like to know about Earth?"

***

A light *bump* jostled Cassidy from sleep. Sharpening her senses against the haze in her mind she opened her eyes, only to be greeted by the back of Aldan's head from the pilot's chair. He powered down the engines. "You gonna make it?"

"I'll do my best," she quipped, a huge yawn splitting her face as she stretched in her seat.

Aldan grinned, and Cassidy felt her face redden at his response.

The porthole whooshed open, and Aldan laughed as he climbed through it with ease. Cassidy followed suit, after she disengaged her safety straps, vaulting herself after him to the ground below.

They were inside a massive mountain crater.

The distinct pattern of the rock was familiar. Cassidy toed at the glassy surface before inspecting the area around them, assessing where Aldan had set down the aircraft. There was no doubt that she was back at the cave system that housed the portals, but their access to the site had come from the air. The open sky that currently stretched above her was not visible from the underground caverns where she'd arrived.

The sound of approaching footfalls made her freeze, and Cassidy turned her attention to Aldan to check on his status.

Aldan ran his fingers through his hair and gave her a cocky grin. "You didn't think we were the only ones here, did you?"

Cassidy said nothing, letting her glare do all the talking.

Aldan pressed his lips together to stifle a laugh.

A pair of Tellurians came into view from the other side of the aircraft. Cassidy was dismayed to see that they wore a uniform similar to the guards from the Government building.

They saluted Aldan before adopting a wide-legged

stance. The woman, the closest soldier to them, rested her hand on the hilt of her holstered weapon while casually keeping Cassidy in her sights.

Aldan assessed the woman, then slid his gaze to the man. "Anything to report?" There was no trace of the usual warmth in his voice.

"Everything is ready on our end, sir. We synthesized fake rockslides and cave-ins to deter the government's search parties from finding the entrance to the caves."

Aldan frowned. "Search parties already? That was fast."

"Yes sir," the woman replied. "It seems they are looking for the missing fugitive and assume she will be returning to the place of capture."

It took Cassidy a moment to realize that the woman's disdain was directed at her. She opened her mouth to reply in kind, but Aldan cut her off before she had the chance.

"Any other activity to report?" When they shook their heads, Aldan nodded. "Very good. I want regular updates—regardless if there's anything to report or not. Keep a low profile. I don't want anyone engaging with the other forces without my say-so. Understood?" He looked satisfied when they nodded. "Dismissed,"

They saluted again and, without so much as a glance to Cassidy, returned to their posts.

"You're military," she said to Aldan, her question coming out as a statement. No wonder he knew what the government did to criminals.

"Ex-military," he corrected, rolling his shoulders. "You didn't think I got by on my rugged good looks, did you?"

He laughed when she gaped at him and strolled over to a projector terminal, activating the device that would hide the base from aerial view.

Ignoring the warmth in her cheeks, Cassidy walked in the opposite direction, curiosity directing her to trudge further into their base of operations. She was careful to avoid the stationed soldiers, opting instead for the glassy paths that snaked deeper into the earth. Small points of light, tiny glowing rocks that were scattered haphazardly along the floors of the tunnels, illuminated the paths like flickering stars in the darkness. It wasn't enough for her to see what was ahead, but they were an excellent way to show where the Tellurians had already been.

Aldan came to stand behind her. "Light markers," he said, nodding to the path ahead. "We can turn them off when necessary, so that they blend into their surroundings."

"Genius," Cassidy replied. "Hansel and Gretel would have had a much easier time with things if they'd used glowing breadcrumbs."

Aldan looked confused. "Did your soldiers deploy without proper reconnaissance gear for their mission?"

Cassidy surprised herself by laughing. The soft sound erupting from her as she dismissed her comment with a wave of her hand. "Something like that." Of course, he wouldn't know Earth fables.

Inspecting the area around them, she tapped her fingers against the cool wall with a soft hum.

"Problem?" Aldan asked in response to the frown that spread across her face.

Cassidy dropped her hand. "I don't know where the

entrance is."

Aldan raised his brows. "Pardon?"

Cassidy gestured around them. "We're up too high. I arrived underground; in a cave that sloped up to the surface. I didn't come into an open-air cavern such as this."

Aldan's frown mirrored her own. "This is the only opening our scout vessels could find that offered us a high enough vantage point against possible attack."

Cassidy cocked her head. "Scout vessels? *Flying* scout vessels...?"

A flicker of exasperation played across Aldan's face, and he pinched the bridge of his nose. "...Which are completely unhelpful if you were found on the ground and not in the air." Aldan pursed his lips in thought, walking slowly back toward the large, illuminated cavern where his aircraft rested, commanding the space of the barren room around it. Barren except for the military supply crates that were grouped together next to the soldiers that were farthest away from the entrance.

"You said that you were picked up by a government patrol car?" he asked, slowing his steps until he became still. When Cassidy nodded, he looked thoughtful. "It will take months for us to explore the entire cave system. The mountains span along the road for a day's drive, and the tunnels stretch between them. But if you could remember a landmark of some sort from where they found you..."

Cassidy racked her brain, sifting through everything that had happened in the past few days. "Not where they found me, no," the whole area had been dried red earth with large rocks and little vegetation, "but before that, yes!" Cassidy felt her heartbeat speed up as she thought back. "There was a section of the road that had cliffs on both sides. The mountain had been blasted in order to create the road. It was the only section like that that I encountered."

"I know exactly where that is," he mused, and Cassidy felt a surge of relief as he continued "but the question is, how do we get down there without being noticed? Patrols are already looking for you."

Cassidy cast her gaze around the cavern again, stopping when her eyes alighted on the tactical gear. She nodded to the harnesses that were stacked next to large coils of thick, woven rope. "How are you at cave rappelling?"

Aldan grinned, and the glint in his eye caused the tips of her fingers to tingle in response.

CHAPTER NINE

Cassidy peered over the lip of the cliff into the darkness below. Her headlamp illuminated a short distance of the open air in front of her, but it did little to assist the yawning descent she was faced with.

It had taken them hours to get this far—tracking their way through an underground labyrinth of paths to get down to where they were now. Several times they had to reclimb a cliff and skirt their way to another opening when they could find no exits from their current plateau.

"Do you see it?" Aldan's voice seemed far away in consuming darkness. The only indication that she was not alone was the flickering of his headlamp as he searched the area.

Cassidy combed the darkness with her gaze until she found the light marker that he tossed into the chasm. "Found it."

"Distance?"

"About 40 feet, give or take."

She heard him grunt in acknowledgement as he did a mental calculation to the Tellurian unit of measurement.

"Sounds great."

"Great!" And, without another moment's hesitation, Cassidy tipped herself over the edge of the rock face and into the gaping chasm below.

"Cassidy!" Aldan yelped, and she could see the light ring of his headlamp pitch forward in an attempt to catch her.

Laughter bubbled out of her as she fell through the darkness. She let the loose, bottom section of the rope run across the palm of her hand, watching the size of the light marker grow at an almost alarming rate as she barrelled toward it. She waited until she judged herself close enough, then activated the Tellurian gripping gloves that Aldan had given her to wear.

Her descent came to an immediate halt as the force shields from the gloves latched onto the thick rope with a sharp jerk. Cassidy grunted at the strain in her arms from the sudden stop. Deactivating the gloves, she slid the remaining ten feet down to rope to the solid rock below.

She heard a thud as Aldan landed several feet away from her. "Are you insane?" he demanded, flustered.

"Sometimes," she acknowledged in a too-cheery tone. Aldan muttered to himself under his breath as he unhooked his harness from the rope with more force than was necessary.

Cassidy unclipped herself and walked the few feet to pick up the light marker. Holding it, she tapped a dial on the back of her glove and felt a small twinge of satisfaction when the fist-sized stone went dark.

They looked around. Their light beams converged at an opening in the rock wall, and Aldan made a noise of satisfaction.

As one, they left their ropes hanging and walked toward the opening across the plateau. "With any luck, this should lead us to the surface," Aldan said in a hushed tone, peering into the dark passageway when they reached it. He tapped his glove and used the illumination from his fingers to scour the darkness.

"It's in the right direction. And it slopes up," Cassidy offered helpfully, eyeing where the wall joined the floor of the tunnel.

Aldan snorted. "Barely."

She took a few steps forward. "It's the best we've got… unless you'd rather climb back up the cliff and look for something else?" She turned back for the last part and was rewarded when he grumbled under his breath and strode past her.

Grinning, she followed him. They travelled in silence for several minutes, the only noise was the scattered water droplets that fell from the rock above them. After a while, the tunnel veered up at a sharp angle. Cassidy, who had been enjoying the chance to stretch her legs with the hike, cursed her previous optimism as she felt a dull burning in her thighs as she attempted to keep up with Aldan's determined pace. She couldn't tell if his hurried stride was for her benefit or his, but she refused to ask him to slow down as they puffed their way toward the surface.

A distant rumbling caused Aldan to snap to attention, halting in his tracks.

Cassidy lurched her body to the side to avoid him, nearly stumbling in her haste. "What—"

"Shh!" He lifted an illuminated finger to his lips.

Biting back a retort, she remained motionless while

Aldan switched off their lights with his gloves. Their head lamps dimmed, and they were plunged into darkness.

Cassidy could see the outline of his form without their equipment. They were close to the surface.

The rumbling became louder. They both looked up as the vibrations shook the ground above them, knocking loose small rocks that rained down around them haphazardly, bouncing between their boots. Aldan shimmied out of his harness and left it and his shoulder pack fall to the ground with a dull thud. Whipping off his overcoat, he gave it a flick and Cassidy was surprised to see that the material snapped into a thin shield that he immediately held over them.

"Patrol vehicles," Aldan whispered over the rumbling.

Huddled together in the darkness, Cassidy was acutely aware of their shoulders touching, and his warm breath against her cheek. Ignoring it, she eyed the trembling rock face above them as the automobiles drove past. They waited in the silence for several minutes before they dared to move. "We must be under the road," Cassidy said, turning. She stopped abruptly, her face inches from his own where he watched her in the dim light.

She felt heat rise to her cheeks, and the tingling feeling in the tips of her fingers returned, but it wasn't from excitement.

Aldan cleared his throat and snapped down the shield, waving it back into an overcoat. He switched their head-lamps back on. "Let's look for an opening," his voice was gruff as he stuffed his harness into his pack and continued up the underground slope.

Cassidy blinked. Rubbing her hands against her legs, she squared her shoulders and followed after him.

She didn't have far to go. There was a slight bend in the tunnel, then a solid rock wall. She assessed the boulders that obstructed their exit to the surface.

"That seems problematic." Cassidy fought the urge to wince when her voice came out more bitter than intended, but she was rewarded when the side of Aldan's mouth quirked up in a smile. "Suggestions?"

Aldan tapped against the rock wall in several places and huffed. "Well, it's not a projection... that means things are about to get loud." He set his backpack on the ground and rummaged inside. He pulled out a small grey blob and jerked his head back the way they came. "Hunker down and get ready to run. We're about to get some unwanted attention."

Cassidy jogged back the way they came, using the bend in the path to shield herself from the impending blast. She covered her ears just as a small explosion rocked the area, sending mid-sized boulders rolling past her from the obstruction.

"Aldan!" she called, rushing forward when he didn't join her. She found him lying on the ground a few feet from the blasting site. He opened his eyes at the sound of her voice and groaned, extending his hand. She grabbed it and pulled him into a standing position.

"That new clay explosive is powerful stuff," he dusted off his pants and made a show of checking that all of his fingers were still attached. "Let's go," he said, when satisfied. "That explosion is certainly going to grab their attention."

Cassidy nodded and took the lead, shifting several of the smaller stones out of the way. Light from the outside world began to filter in through the cracks. She redoubled her efforts, digging at the stones and pushing them out of the way behind her in a small pile. Aldan joined in next to her.

The opening became wide enough to squeeze though. Cassidy pushed herself through the small opening, twisting her body to fit the small space as she climbed around the boulders that were too heavy to move. Once free, she stood a moment to appreciate the warm sun on her face and the fresh breeze in her hair.

"Here," Aldan hissed behind her. She grabbed his offered pack and slung it over a shoulder while he crawled through the opening. She felt better for wearing it. She didn't realize how much she had been missing hers since the Tellurian government had confiscated it. He grinned as he stepped onto the dark red clay of the moon's surface.

He shielded his eyes with a hand and surveyed the area. "Perfect. This is exactly where I wanted to be."

Cassidy rolled her eyes at his smug tone but said nothing.

"You should have come out of the portal around here," he told her, his eyes dragging along the road that cut diagonally in front of them through the outcropping of the rocky mountain. "Now, we just have to determine the direction you..."

Cassidy turned her attention to him when he trailed off. He was peering into the distance, head cocked as if listening for something. "Aldan? What is it?"

He shushed her and remained motionless.

Cassidy stepped around him and strained her eyes to see what he was looking at. She saw nothing but an empty stretch of road that dipped into the horizon. She frowned and was about to open her mouth to admonish him for shushing her, but then movement caught her eye. A cloud of red dust had formed in the distance, and it was growing fast. She watched it, letting her senses focus as it spread across the road and came toward them. Her ears picked up on the muted rumblings of an approaching engine before her feet felt them.

The patrol had heard the explosion, and they were coming to investigate.

Aldan swore under his breath. "We've got to move. Now."

As one, they ran across the road, putting as much distance between them and the obvious blast site as quickly as possible. They threw themselves behind a rocky outcropping while looking for the best place to climb.

Aldan swore again. "The ropes are still hanging where we left them."

"Alert the camp," Cassidy told him. It would take hours for the officers to backtrack through the tunnels to where they had started, possibly even days if they could do it at all, but there was no need to risk it. "I'll look for a place to hide."

Aldan touched the communicator that he wore in his ear while Cassidy scrambled along the base of the ridge to look for a place for them to hide.

Cassidy hurried ahead, scouting for a cave they could duck into when something caught her eye. A small footprint, shrunken into the clay-like ground, led away from the wall of rock and toward the road. Cassidy recognized it as her own from when she originally squeezed out of the cave system into the dark night of Telluria.

"Aldan!"

Aldan jerked his head toward her at her shout. Tapping his earpiece to finish his transmission, he sprinted toward her, nimbly weaving around the rocky outcroppings in an attempt to reach her before the vehicles arrived.

"You found it?" he asked, barely winded as he reached the edge of the footprint. When she nodded, he slid sideways through the opening, extending a hand to help her in after him. "Lead the way." he told her, his voice soft in the small space.

Cassidy nodded and squeezed past him. Retracing her steps with ease, they strode deeper into the mountain.

The rumbling behind them became louder and Cassidy quickened her pace. The scout teams were almost at the entrance to the tunnel.

They arrived at a fork in the road that Cassidy didn't remember, and Aldan collided with her when she paused without warning to inspect it. "What's wrong?"

"This wasn't here last time." She swept her light between the paths that branched off in different directions.

"I thought you said this was the entrance..."

"It is. This is the way I came out."

She could see him frown as he raked his gaze along the walls around them. He squinted, as if trying to make something out. "I don't think there are any projections present..."

The rumbling grew louder. Cassidy felt her heart

speed up as the vehicles came to a halt in front of the hidden entrance. To her surprise, Aldan stepped toward her and gripped her shoulders. With the slightest push of his fingers, he directed her to turn and face the way they came, then pulled her so she took several steps back.

They stood without moving. Cassidy was aware of the light pressure of his fingertips against the sides of her shoulders, and the sounds of the soldiers' boots hitting the ground outside. "Look again," he told her, his voice calming the distractions around them.

The low light through the tiny entrance illuminated the way that she had taken last time. When she'd stumbled from the side-tunnel, connecting with the main one that led to the exit.

Of course, there was no fork in the road. It had been behind her when she arrived. She hadn't noticed the transition because of the number the portal had done on her vision.

"I must really be tired," she muttered with a sigh, taking a step into the tunnel on their now-left.

Aldan chuckled and relieved her of the pack, rummaging in it and pulling out one of the projection shield devices that Cassidy recognized from the underground base. "Go ahead and find the portal. I'll buy us some time," he told her, attaching the device to the outside corner.

Cassidy nodded. She had only travelled several steps before the air around her thickened and she felt the familiar pull of the portal.

Not every portal felt the same. Many didn't offer any warning, so Cassidy was relieved that she was able to find this one with relative ease.

The sound of shouting interrupted her thoughts. A small explosion caused her to stumble, and she heard Aldan curse behind her. The soldiers had blown apart the opening of the tunnel and were heading toward them.

"Run," he told her, as the force shield flickered to life. The projection knit along itself from the rock wall and into the air between them. "I'll distract them while the shield forms. The others in the Resistance will find you. You must get more of the growing agent—"

"Not without you," she interrupted, dismissing his plan of self-sacrifice. Lurching forward, she grabbed his arm and yanked him toward her with all her strength.

They lost their footing and stumbled backward.

The projection completely obstructed the entrance to the tunnel. Even as she felt the air thicken around them, as they fell backward into the portal, Cassidy hoped that it had formed in time to throw the search party off their path.

CHAPTER TEN

Cassidy grunted as her back slammed into the ground. Above her, Aldan caught himself as he fell on top of her, a grunt escaping his lips with the sudden exertion.

They paused there a moment, staring at each other. His eyes were wide with the shock at the sensation of being transported through a portal.

Snapping out of it, he scrambled to his feet, offering her his hand. "Are you okay?" he asked, his headlamp sputtering as he checked her over.

She accepted his help and he pulled her to her feet with ease. "I'm fine. You?" When he nodded, she exhaled in relief. Their pursuers had not followed them through the portal, so she could only assume that the force shield had activated in time.

His expression of relief turned into annoyance. "That was a foolish thing to do."

"Nonsense. I'm never foolish." Cassidy bit back a grin at the glare he shot her. "Besides, I can't get around Alluvia without you."

He snorted, looking mollified, then gestured ahead of them. "After you."

Cassidy strolled ahead, noting the familiarity of the tunnel as she unhooked her climbing harness. This was going to be easier than she thought.

Sunlight bounced off the shiny walls of the cave that widened at the end of the tunnel, reflecting on the glass-like rock that had formed around the portal. She wondered momentarily which came first—the cave or the portal—and made a note to bring the question up with Gamgee when she returned home.

Home...

The acrid chemical smell of the atmosphere invaded her senses. It started as a tingle in her nose, then crept down her throat the longer she continued to breathe it in.

Behind her, Aldan started to cough.

"Welcome to Alluvia," she murmured, stepping from the dark cave into the harsh light of the toxic sun.

***

The acrid smell of chemicals snaked its way up her nose and down her throat, causing her to cough as she spoke. Vinegar and rotting vegetation. She hadn't missed that combination. "Now what?"

Aldan's reaction to the smell was worse. He was very obviously trying not to gag as he surveyed the area around them with watering eyes. "Now we wait for our underground operative to make contact," Aldan told her, his voice straining with the effort of suppressing a cough.

Cassidy didn't know if it was his heightened senses, or the fact that his planet was virtually pollution-free, that was giving him such a hard time transitioning to the new atmosphere, but she knew that he had to get inside somewhere—and soon.

"C'mon," Cassidy zipped her coat up and tucked her nose under the collar. She nodded when Aldan followed suit and zipped his collar up over the lower-half of his face. "The dome is up ahead. Let's get you out of the atmosphere."

Slipping into the dome proved easier this time around. Cassidy had led them around to the back of the rock dome, returning to the exit which didn't have the sensors at the front that had alerted the Alluvians to her original arrival and had caused them to launch the automated vehicle that had picked her up. She could only assume that the lack of security was because of the proximity to the other domes that connected in that area.

Cassidy tucked her flaming red hair under a hat—her colouring was closer to the Alluvian's than Aldan's, but her hair would certainly give away the difference—and Aldan paused to smear a pale pigment all over his face. It wasn't quite strong enough, but he could pass for Alluvian so long as no one looked too closely. She held her breath, and the two slipped into the market and joined the crowd of the citizens who were casually strolling between the yellow-orange buildings of the dome.

"Must be lunch time," Cassidy muttered, reminded of the way the campus courtyards filled between classes back on Earth.

The scent of cooking food assaulted their senses, and as one they turned toward the source. A small stand, something akin to a permanent food truck, stood in front of an open-air cooking pit, where the source of the delicious smells was wafting toward them from the automated rotisserie.

Aldan pulled several coins out of his breast pocket and clinked them together in his palm. "In the meantime…"

Cassidy didn't bother asking where he had secured the Alluvian currency. One of his Resistance contacts likely slipped it into transport shipment. Instead, she ordered for them by pointing at the pictured squares on the menu, choosing the combos that were displayed on the beaten plastic sign. Aldan kept his eyes downcast, avoiding meeting the worker's gaze so that his eye colour would not be noticed.

When they received the food, Aldan led the way to an outdoor seating area. He looked as exhausted as she felt, and Cassidy realized that it had been countless hours since either of them had rested.

They ate the food in silence while Aldan assessed the area.

The courtyard was unchanged since her last visit. The red rock of the dome, fortified by the same material she had witnessed a few days ago in the lab, sheltered the Alluvians from their toxic environment. She watched as Aldan ran his gaze up the storeys of yellow buildings to where their heights disappeared against the protection of the dome. Cassidy dragged her gaze to the tunnel that led to the formal garden, and spent a wistful moment wishing she could show Aldan the beautiful trees that grew there. Giving herself a shake, she returned her attention to the space around them.

The hairs on the back of Cassidy's neck prickled. She rubbed at them, looking for the source. There was no wind in this controlled environment, so something else must be causing it.

Her eyes fell on a man seated outside a cafe. He was dressed in the same red clothing that many of the Alluvian's wore, his close-clipped shock of bright orange hair standing out against the red rock that surrounded them. The color was so bright it was almost comical, and it clashed horribly with the red he wore. He was slowly sipping on a hot beverage, looking all the world like a relaxed Earth college student, but the intensity in which he surveyed his surroundings sent a tingle down Cassidy's spine.

"You gonna finish that?" Aldan eyed her half-eaten food. His plate looked as though it had been licked clean, and Cassidy remembered that—other than fish—meat was considered a luxury on Telluria.

"Depends," she countered, pulling her attention back to their table. She turned her body so that the man couldn't see her face. "Can you eat and walk?"

Aldan grinned. "Of course. I'm very accomplished." They rose and he piled her leftover meat onto a square bun with ease. Cassidy gathered the plates and disposed of them in a waste reciprocal as they walked past.

"The building you want is up ahead," she murmured, moving close to him in the public space. She didn't know what the workweek was like—or if they even had a workweek—so she tried her best to emulate the people around her, while also keeping their conversation low enough to avoid any possible eavesdropping.

They had hidden their coloring to the best of their abilities, but there was no need to draw any unnecessary attention.

"Last time you were there you had an escort, yes?" Aldan asked between chews. Cassidy nodded, knowing that he had reread her debriefing file before they left. "Then let's explore on our own and see what we can find."

Cassidy could hear his unspoken meaning. They would wait and see when it was at its most deserted before they attempted anything.

They wove their way toward the facility while Aldan ate. No one took notice of them as they walked, and Cassidy felt herself begin to relax. It wasn't much further to their destination. It wasn't much longer until she was able to go home....

The thought caused her to turn her attention to Aldan, and the unexpected sorrow she felt. She would be leaving him behind. He did say he wanted to see Earth, but...

The thought emptied out of her head, and she stopped in her tracks. There, ahead of them, was the same man who had been watching them outside the cafe. The one with the bright-orange hair.

Aldan took a step forward. His hard gaze was trained on the man in front of them. "Why have you been following us?"

Cassidy felt her eyebrows raise. Had Aldan noticed him tracking them this entire time?

The man reached into his pocket and pulled out a small black device. Cassidy opened her mouth to shout a warning, but it was too late. He pressed the large red button on the device before either of them could react.

Cassidy held her breath.

Nothing happened.

There was a click, and then a red light—the same

shade as the button under the man's thumb—began flashing on Aldan's gloves. Cassidy watched as his posture visibly relaxed.

The man stepped forward with a nod. "Aldan, I presume? I'm Nyler, your contracted tour guide. I've been waiting for you."

CHAPTER ELEVEN

"I came early," Nyler said, leading them out of the public space and down a side alley. Buildings crowded around them, competing for space as they stretched up to the curved rock of the dome. The artificial sunlight was not as bright in the alley. "I wanted to make sure you weren't being followed before we connected."

Cassidy nodded. "Smart."

Nyler inclined his head, casting her a curious glance even as he led the way. "You are Cassidy Cane. The unexpected visitor who arrived on our planet last week." They were statements more than questions. When she nodded in response, he looked amused. "From the stories, I was picturing someone… taller."

Aldan covered a laugh with a cough and did his best to look innocent when she cast him a look.

"I can assure you that my short stature has no bearing on my capabilities," she replied, her tone indicating that she was speaking to both men.

A slow smile slid across Nyler's face. "Of that I have no doubt."

They fell silent as a group of school-aged children

passed them. Cassidy could see Aldan's expression as they passed, his eyes questioning as he watched the children as they hurried toward the courtyard together. Their skin looked ghastly pale in the dim lighting, a stark contrast to the colorful rock that surrounded them. They panted, struggling to fill their lungs with air at their quick pace. It was apparent that they were all several meals away from being considered underweight.

Aldan's expression was unreadable.

"What's the plan?" Cassidy asked Nyler once the children were out of earshot, hoping to distract Aldan out of whatever spiral his mind was taking and to restore his attention to the job at hand.

Nyler motioned up ahead. Cassidy could see the narrow alley widen again into a larger area, with several commercial buildings hugging the pathways. "A work crew is scheduled to arrive in the next few hours. They're on contract to conduct repairs to the air filtration system in the research facility."

"Big job," Aldan noted. Cassidy nodded in agreement, remembering the outside atmosphere and the lengths the citizens took to keep it outside of the safe zones.

"Big job, and an excellent opportunity to walk into the facility unnoticed."

Aldan frowned. "I assume we'll need credentials for that..."

"...which you will be providing?" Cassidy continued, noting that the end of the square had another seal to the outside planet, much like the one that they entered through. The difference was that this one seemed less inviting. No civilians milled around the barrier, and posted guards were checking ID bracelets of the people who were entering from the secure area.

Nyler nodded and led them to an adjacent building. The ease with which he navigated through the empty building had her breathing a sigh of relief.

"Here," he said, unlocking a small, windowless room and flicking on the lights so they could enter. When Aldan stared at him, refusing to move, Nyler rolled his eyes and stepped into the room first. "Fair enough," Cassidy heard him mutter.

She stepped into the room and looked around. It was a cross between a storage room and a locker room. Miscellaneous items were pushed against the wall—stacked chairs and broken benches—items so painfully boring that Cassidy was impressed by the ingenuity of the planet's small resistance faction. They hid well in plain sight.

Nyler unlocked one of the vertical cabinets and pulled out several hanging outfits for Aldan and Cassidy to try on. They reminded her of cloth coveralls from Earth, but instead of one large zipper to secure them, they automatically cinched to their bodies, folding in on themselves until they were secure around their waists, arms, and necks.

Cassidy pulled at the fabric around her neck, dismayed that it had less give than a turtleneck. "Is this really necessary?"

"Only if you want to get into the facility without detection. I can smell the atmosphere off of you from here. This should help to cover it. Besides," he nodded to Aldan, "your compound is about to wear off. I can see your skin tone breaking through."

He was right. The pigment cream that Aldan had used

had already started to decay from the chemicals of the atmosphere, and she could see patches of his red skin peeking through like rusty undertones. Cassidy sighed but said nothing. This was their show. A deal was a deal. She was so accustomed to working alone—sneaking into places after dark, or climbing into ancient sites to retrieve priceless artifacts—that the idea of waltzing into a restricted destination with a crowd of people during the day seemed completely foreign to her. More foreign than jumping through invisible portals onto alien worlds, somehow.

Nyler popped open a hidden drawer at the back of the locker. "I'll go check and see when the repair team arrives. We'll join them when they do." He tossed them each an ID bracelet before closing the locker. "Put these on. It's unlikely that everyone will be scanned again so soon after arrival, but you might as well look the part."

Aldan frowned and snapped the bracelet over his wrist. There was a humming sound, and it retracted into itself until it sat flush against his skin. A pale purple light began to blink along the top. "And if they do decide to scan everyone again?"

Nyler grinned. "Improvise."

CHAPTER TWELVE

Cassidy resisted the urge to tug at her uniform. Instead, she kept her arms clamped to her sides as she marched with Aldan and Nyler and the rest of the repair crew into the large government building. Guards in brick-red uniforms stood posted at the entranceway, a precaution that had been implemented since Cassidy had last been there, scanning the crowd intermittently as the workers entered through the automated doors. She hastily scoured the area around her and was relieved that there were no familiar faces present.

Not that they would recognize her dressed like this. None of the work crew's faces were visible around their masks.

Last time Elona had led her through a small side-corridor. This time she entered through the front door. They marched into the foyer, the double doors hissed shut behind them with a finality that Cassidy felt in her spine. She would be glad when she could put this place behind her.

"Team A, you're to work on the 8th Floor," a voice boomed from the front of the room, causing everyone to become still. "Team B, Section 1: you're to go to the 11th Floor; Section 2: the basement." There was grumbling around them, but the director clapped their hands. "Move out, people. Those atmospheric leaks aren't going to fix themselves."

"C'mon," she motioned to Aldan and followed after Section 1. An elevator, much different from the secure, open-air one she had used last time, waited ahead of them. Cassidy waved her hand over the scanner and it answered with a musical chime as the elevator moved down to their floor. "Going up," she called out, inserting her hand into the door sensor after it arrived in order to keep it open. "11th Floor. After you. I insist."

Aldan watched her, wide-eyed, as she verbally herded Section 1 into the machine. "Squeeze in. There you go." Nyler gave her a nod from the elevator, and she removed her hand. The door slid closed with a warning bell. "You go ahead! We'll catch the next one. Yes, I insist. Thanks so much!"

Multiple pairs of eyes watched her with surprise between their safety masks as the door closed between them. Cassidy chuckled and turned to Aldan, who was also staring at her in surprise. "Lemmings."

Aldan looked perplexed. "What?"

"Never mind," she replied, remembering they were an Earth animal. She waited until the elevator was several floors up before running her hand through the scanner. An answering ding lit up the indicator, and a second elevator responded to her summons.

The door whooshed open, and they stepped inside. Aldan frowned at all the options. "I assume you know where you're going."

Cassidy pressed the button to the top floor without hesitation. "I have a very good memory."

"And if you're wrong?"

Cassidy gave a smirk, adjusting her hat and checking that her red hair stayed concealed. "Then we'll improvise."

Aldan muttered something under his breath that she couldn't quite make out, but from his tone she could tell that it wasn't flattering. She gave a soft laugh and he grinned in response.

A gentle chime announced their arrival and they sobered instantly. The door opened into a dark corridor, and Cassidy could feel Aldan shift his weight as he pressed a hand against his thigh. She knew he carried some sort of concealed weapon, but she had assumed it was in the pack that he'd refused to relinquish to Nyler in the storage room.

At least he came prepared.

The two stepped onto the floor, Cassidy mincing behind Aldan as he took the lead.

"According to our intel, there's a main computer that can access all the schematic databases." His voice was hushed in the dark hallway.

Cassidy knew which room he was talking about. "The war room," she confirmed. When he looked at her in surprise, she nodded ahead of them to the lone door in the corridor. The lift that she had taken last time on the other side of it. "I've been here already."

Aldan surveyed the locked door. He peered at the screen next to it, eyes narrowing as he tried to make sense of the shifting colors. "I wasn't expecting this type of lock-ing mechanism," he said at last.

"The code was a rainbow pattern," Cassidy offered, feeling unhelpful at best. Surprisingly, this seemed to mean something to him, and he keyed in a few different codes before it accepted one of them.

The door clicked open and swung inward.

"Paydirt," she told Aldan.

Aldan gave her a strange look, his expression clearly skeptical as he assessed her cognitive abilities. "It's not dirt, it's a growing agent. And we want the computer the information is stored on—"

Cassidy resisted the urge to sigh and stepped back. "Whatever it is, it's in there."

Aldan rolled his eyes and toed the door open further with his boot. The room was silent and dark, save for a few lights that flashed on one of the consoles that lined the walls. As they walked across the floor, large fluores-cent lights popped into existence above them. Cassidy led the way to a giant desk that commanded the room. She frowned at the dark surface of the desk. Without the lights, it looked like an ordinary meeting table.

"What..." she frowned and looked around its base for a hint of wires or plugs. "I swear this is it."

Aldan said nothing and scanned the room.

"Aren't you going to help?" She demanded, exasper-ated.

"Help poke at the giant machine that obviously isn't doing the one thing it's supposed to be doing in the only place it's supposed to be?" he drawled, ignoring the glare she shot at him as he continued to inspect the floor. His eyes ran along a perpendicular seam in the carpet that intersected with the corner of the desk. He smirked. "Sure."

Cassidy pressed her fists into her hips and watched as he made a show of walking along the carpet seam where it met the table. Finding nothing, he probed the raised fabric with a finger, then, to her surprise, peeled back that section of the carpet to uncover a coiled wire that connected to the table.

Making a noise of satisfaction in his throat, he tapped a dial on his glove and pressed a finger into the wire. An electrical jolt passed from his glove and sparked along the metal and into the table.

There was a click, then the sound of moving gears as a section of the tabletop moved and an internal compartment raised the large screen into view.

Cassidy stepped forward. "Clever."

Aldan reached around her and began waving a hand over the screen. His fingers activated unseen sensors, and Cassidy watched as Aldan navigated seamlessly through invisible settings to flip through various folders on the machine.

The muted chime of an arriving elevator broke the silence. Cassidy felt the back of her neck prickle and she turned her attention to the hallway. "Aldan," she warned.

Aldan looked up with a grimace. "I need more time."

Cassidy sucked in a quick breath while her mind raced. Giving a nod, she sprinted to the open door and closed it carefully, holding the thick metal door as best she could so that it closed with the barest click of the latch.

The locking mechanism clicked.

The lights dimmed in response, and Cassidy crouched down out of habit.

Aldan did the same, placing the desk between himself and the hallway, but continued sorting through the files to find what he was looking for.

There was the sound of approaching footsteps, and Cassidy held her breath as she heard the guards spread out along the hallway.

There was a rattling of the doorknob, but the door didn't budge.

"Check the alarm system," a gruff voice commanded. "I'm positive this was the office that was set off." The guard tried the door again to no avail.

Cassidy crept toward Aldan as the guards prowled toward the back elevator. He'd placed a small device on the monitor and was watching it as the light on it blinked at an intermittent tempo.

"Now would be a good time to go," she hissed.

"Not yet," he murmured, watching as the light sped up.

They both looked up as footsteps rushed down the hall.

"Now," Cassidy insisted.

Aldan flicked his eyes to the triangular device. The blinking light had become one solid color as the information transfer finished. "Let's go."

He snatched the transfer stick from the terminal just as the door swung open. "Not that way," he pivoted toward the back of the room.

Cassidy stared at him and the wall of windows behind them. "What..." but she had no time to finish her question. He grabbed her hand as he ran past, pulling her with him. "They don't open!" she protested, moving with him. This floor was high enough that it was above the confines of the dome. Cassidy guessed that they had found it easier to fortify this area of the building instead of raising the rocky barrier to its height.

Aldan secured his pack over his shoulders with his free hand, clipping the straps together across his chest. "Then we'll have to open them."

They stopped at the large windows. Aldan pulled a wire from his pack and secured it around the sturdy atmospheric pipes at the base of the window, then he pressed a thin disc to the glass—the same type of device he used for the door—turning it so that it stuck to the surface. He tapped it, and it began to emit a high-pitched whine. Cassidy backed up as thin cracks spread out of the disc like glistening spiderwebs.

The war room door was kicked open and the guards poured into the room.

"Let's go!" Aldan grabbed her hand and pulled her against him. His arms around her were strong as he held her tight against him. He turned so that their backs were to the glass. "Brace yourself!"

Before Cassidy could respond, Aldan launched them against the window with a powerful push of his legs. He grunted at the impact, but the glass remained intact.

Despite herself, a laugh bubbled out of Cassidy at the absurdity of the situation. She could feel Aldan's flaming cheek next to hers and she began to laugh in earnest.

"Very funny," he muttered.

Cassidy didn't know if it was her lack of sleep that

was driving her reaction, or his embarrassment at the failed escape attempt, but another laugh escaped her lips. "S-sorry."

Aldan huffed and peered over her shoulder at his gloves. He tapped the activator button and the disc behind them caused the glass to pop. "I was distracted," he muttered, pulling her close.

Cassidy felt her heartbeat speed up.

The guards took their positions. "Stop right there!" The commander ordered. "You're under arrest!"

"Only if you catch us." Aldan taunted, launching them against the window.

This time the glass broke on contact.

A breathless scream escaped Cassidy's lips as they plummeted through the open air. Panic gripped her mind until the sound of the extending metal cord filled her ears. She willed herself to calm down even as her fingers bit into Aldan's arm in a death-grip.

Spelunking. They were just spelunking.

Large shards of glass from the window clinked harmlessly off of her face mask. The smaller pieces had been sucked into the room from the force of the vacuum that Aldan had created. Whether it had been strategic or not she didn't know, but it had done the trick. The guards' screams followed them as they fell. The horror apparent in their tone as the noxious atmosphere rushed into the room where they stood.

At least they were too busy to attempt to break their metal lifeline.

Cassidy shut out the sound of their voices. Instead, she concentrated on the rocky top of the atmospheric dome as they plummeted toward it.

They were falling at an incredible speed.

Aldan's arms were locked tight around her. Cassidy craned her neck around and called his name, but he ignored her. Instead of watching the spooling metal line, or the quickly-approaching rocky red surface, his eyes were glued to the passing windows. She watched as his eyes darted from one window to the next, his gaze hurriedly flicked over the panes of glass as they fell.

What was he looking for?

Cassidy's heart pounded. She faced forward and scanned the windows. The outline of their falling form was reflected back at her in the glass. The light was bright enough that she could barely see into the rooms if she adjusted her focus, but nothing of any consequence stood out at her. No glaringly-obvious sign of what Aldan was looking for.

Except...

She jerked her head to the side. The relentless sun sliced into a fractured spiderweb. There, sitting in the middle of the stretching faucets, was a thin metal disc. A suggestion of a shadow that hung as a sign of their salvation.

"There!" Cassidy pointed with a scream.

Aldan's reaction was immediate. He clenched a fist and the metal wire snapped with the tension of their weight. He grunted in her ear, arms locked around her as the give in the rope disappeared, his pack acting like a harness similar to the ones they had used to scale down the cliffs earlier.

Cassidy had twined her legs around his, determined that there was no way she would allow him to drop her.

She didn't have to worry. The abrupt halt in their descent caused them to swing toward the building. Aldan lifted his legs—and Cassidy's—in front of them and angled his feet so that the heels of his boots made the first impact. They hit their mark, slamming into the metal disc with the full force of their combined weights, causing the fractured window to shatter around them as they were thrown into the room.

At some point they became untangled from each other. Cassidy flew ahead of him into the room. She caught herself by rolling across the plush carpet to spread out the impact of her landing. Her mask, the side strap sliced through from the jagged window, flew off of her face with the movement. She came to a halt on her back, splayed only a few feet away from where Aldan was groaning. The tingling in her fingers had nothing to do with how tightly she had gripped the straps around his chest. She propped herself up on an elbow to assess him, grinning when he groaned again, then flopped back over to catch her breath.

With her head cushioned against the floor, and nothing but the sound of their labored breathing filling the room, Cassidy couldn't help herself as the absurdity of the situation caught up with her.

She laughed.

There was an edge of tension to it that she didn't quite feel, as if her own hysteria was hiding from her somehow. The sound of it set her off even more, and before she knew it, tears were streaming down her face as laughter peeled out of her

She tried to control herself, only to realize that Aldan

had joined in and was laughing right along with her. Or maybe it was at her. She couldn't tell, and she certainly didn't care.

A helmeted head appeared over her and Nyler looked down at Cassidy with raised eyebrows. "Having fun?" he asked the two of them.

Cassidy's only response was a hiccup, and the sound was enough to push Aldan into another fit of laughter that had Nyler shaking his head in disbelief.

CHAPTER THIRTEEN

Nyler helped Aldan and Cassidy to their feet. Cassidy could see the smirk that had settled on his face through the window in his mask. His dark eyes appraised them, focusing on the pack that Aldan had secured over his chest. An eyebrow raised in surprise, but he said nothing, and Cassidy could see that he understood why Aldan had refused to leave his pack at the storage locker.

There was a heartbeat of silence, and Nyler's eyes widened. His gaze darted between Cassidy and the broken window, and the obvious noxious atmosphere funneling into the room with a force that was strong enough to cause her hair to shift with the movement.

Nyler's expression was filled with awe. "So it is true," he breathed.

Cassidy realized that he wasn't staring at her hair color but at her face. At the space where her mask used to rest, and the ease of her breath without it.

He flicked his attention to Aldan, who had come to stand beside her like a supportive shadow. "I had heard the rumors but didn't believe... She can breathe the atmosphere..." When Aldan nodded, Nyler's expression shifted from shock to surprise. "As can you."

Aldan shifted a shoulder in a half-shrug. "Mostly," he conceded. His breath came easier than before, and Cassidy assumed the face mask blocked some of the chemicals that were swirling around them—a small measure of what Nyler's breathing mask could do.

"How?" the Alluvian demanded.

"His body has adapted," Cassidy replied, with a gentleness that she hoped matched the edge in Nyler's voice. "Tellurians function in their atmosphere without assistance. Their physiological changes mean increased lung strength and size for survival on their moon—something that helps on your planet."

The desperation on Nyler's face was apparent even with his breathing mask. "Could that happen for us as well?"

"Eventually…" Aldan stepped forward at the crack of emotion in the other man's voice. "That is our hope." His voice was low. "We want future generations to work together instead of against one another, so that they can create a life that benefits and heals both our peoples. But to accomplish this we will need the continued support of the Alluvian Resistance. We can't do it alone."

Cassidy stared at Aldan after his heart-felt speech, barely recognizing him without the swagger that seemed to be his default setting. She felt a knot loosen in her stomach, and for the first time since her initial arrival through the portal, she didn't feel stupid for being tricked by the Alluvians. Maybe it was something that needed to happen. Maybe it was the catalyst for their peoples finally working together.

Nyler stepped forward and extended a hand, clasping Aldan's forearm. "Then help you shall have."

A grin broke across Aldan's face. Usually, his expressions were filled with self-assured arrogance, but this one was colored with such relief and joy that Cassidy couldn't help but smile in response.

The relief was short-lived. Emergency lights flashed and a grating whine cut through the air. It was all Cassidy could do to keep from clapping her hands over her ears.

"Starting now," Nyler continued, as though the building hadn't burst into high alert. "That isn't related to the atmospheric leaks. Let's get you and that precious technology back to Telluria."

"Fantastic." Aldan glanced behind them at the smashed window, then at the interior of the building where the alarm continued its shrill warning. "How, exactly?"

Nyler frowned but Cassidy stepped forward. "Through the front door." When both men turned to her, brows raised with expectation, she flashed them a grin. "I have a plan, and I think it's going to be a lot of fun."

Nyler looked hopeful, but Aldan took one look at the glint in her eye and groaned.

***

"I thought you said this was going to be fun," Aldan hissed at her, adjusting his position so that the barrel of the blaster was no longer digging into his spine.

"I meant for me," Cassidy clarified, nudging him forward with the weapon.

Aldan and Nyler held their hands high in surrender, marching before her toward the sterile-looking foyer.

Cassidy had discarded her worker's uniform in favour of her usual clothing and Aldan's pack, the only addition to her regular outfit. She had even unbound her hair, letting the snarls of curls—unkempt from days of adventuring—flow past her shoulders, flaunting her identity.

She didn't want any doubt who was terrorizing the Alluvian facility. And with any luck, Aldan and Nyler would appear as nothing but two faceless hostages.

She could hear the sound of people running toward them. She kept their pace unhurried, strutting across the massive stone lobby, maneuvering around the piles of dust and debris that were the result of the different explosions.

Security guards burst into the foyer. They lined off along the walls, shouting at the three as they trained their weapons on them.

Cassidy ignored them and kept moving.

"Don't shoot! Don't shoot!" Nyler and Aldan screamed, waving their hands in a show of desperation.

"Stop now or we'll open fire," roared an officer, stepping forward.

Cassidy's pulse quickened at the sound of her voice. The female officer had put herself between them and the door, but even from this distance, Cassidy recognized the strands of vibrant fuchsia hair that had escaped from the officer's black cap.

Elona.

Cassidy had considered the woman a friend of sorts when she first arrived. That was before the plan for her to sabotage the Tellurian crop had been formed. Before she discovered that Elona had been part of the deception that had sent Cassidy into certain death.

Elona's face had the same smooth, unreadable expression that it held when they first met. The only difference was that her pale purple eyes now pleaded with her to stop. She had never wanted to harm Cassidy. She had been following orders.

Cassidy slowed enough to show that she'd heard the command. Enough so that the others in front of her stopped moving. She had no intention of surrendering. If the Alluvians had planned to kill her for helping them, she didn't want to know what they would do to her for breaking their laws.

The thought strengthened her resolve. The area was silent. Cassidy made a show of lifting her hand and tapping her chest. "I wouldn't do that if I were you," she cautioned.

She felt the room's attention shift to where she tapped. Cassidy partially unzipped her coat and peeled back the outer layer. The room immediately felt tense as she displayed the clay explosives strapped to her chest.

A shove of her blaster into Nyler and Aldan's backs had them doing the same and they showed off their matching devices.

"Shoot any of us and this entire building blows." Cassidy's voice rang easily in the silence.

Elona's eyes widened. She raised a fist to the unit around them in a command to hold their positions. Then, after a long, assessing look at Cassidy, she begrudgingly stepped out of the way.

Cassidy inclined her head and nudged her hostages forward. She raised her other hand to show off the remote detonator she held, her thumb hovering against the triggering button. "Don't even think about shooting me in the back!"

Elona cursed behind her as they exited the building...

...And came face-to-face with a squadron of soldiers.

Aldan and Nyler swore under their breath. Cassidy was unable to join them as the sight of the brick-red wall of uniformed military personnel surrounding them had caused her mouth to go dry.

Large armored vehicles blocked their path. Unlike the automated one that she had used for transit outside of the dome, these ones were not air-tight, and clearly meant for driving on the smooth paved streets. They spread out in a u-shape, the apex of which sat opposite the doors of the building they had just exited. Countless soldiers stood in position between them, and Cassidy scanned the surrounding area for any activity.

Her steps faltered when she noted the snipers in position in the adjacent buildings. Her brain immediately conjured possible scenarios as to how this standoff would end—none of them in her favour—but she kept her gaze focused on the men in front of her and the road ahead of them.

"You better know what you're doing," Nyler mumbled, the slight tremble in his raised hands the only sign of his nervousness.

"Trust us," Aldan whispered back, though Cassidy could hear a twinge of uncertainty in his voice that she hoped Nyler couldn't detect.

"We stick to the plan," she murmured, hoping her

voice projected a confidence that she didn't feel.

The crackle of a radio signal caught her attention. She met the dead-eyed stare of the blue-haired Captain Kruz as he lifted his head away from the communicator at his shoulder. His eyes flicked between the detonation device and the explosives they wore on their chests, and his lip curled in disgust as he took a step back.

Good, Cassidy thought. She felt a twinge of guilt at the expression on his face. She had met him previously while here—as well as his wife and young daughter—and she knew he was thinking of the threat she represented to his family.

Cassidy took a moment before steeling her spine. It didn't matter how he felt so long as he gave them their space.

"Lead the way," she commanded Nyler, her voice harsh. He marched them down the road and between the armoured vehicles, between the soldiers and the weapons they had trained on their bodies.

Cassidy made sure to keep the detonation device in full view.

Nyler unerringly led them to the square where they'd first entered the dome.

"It's empty," Aldan noted, his voice soft as he scanned the area.

Cassidy attempted to swallow past the dryness in her mouth. He was right. The area that had initially been so full of life when they arrived was now silent and deserted. The authorities had evacuated everyone once the alarm was activated, and that was either very good or very bad news for Cassidy.

"I don't like the look of this," Nyler muttered, confirming Cassidy's fear. "They're planning something."

"So are we," Cassidy countered with false bravado. She couldn't argue. There was no reason to evacuate such a large area next to the exit unless they were up to something.

Cassidy could hear the armoured vehicles following at a distance. She spared a glance behind her and was greeted by the sight of the entire squadron inching along after them.

"We've got company," Aldan warned.

Cassidy jerked her attention forward and watched as another squadron of soldiers blocked off the entries to the side streets. With their weapons cocked, she couldn't help but feel as though they were herding them toward the exit.

Aldan twisted his head to the side, his eyes narrowing when he caught sight of the armed gauntlet. "Not good."

"We don't have much of a choice," Cassidy replied through gritted teeth.

"Maybe you don't," Nyler murmured, "but I do."

Before she could respond, the Alluvian began to scream. Everyone jerked to attention at the sound, then tensed as Nyler ran—still screaming—away from Cassidy and toward the nearest armoured car.

Cassidy stared after him, dumbfounded.

"Grab me," Aldan hissed at her.

"What?"

"You're the Tellurian Terrorist—act like it. *Grab me.*"

That was all she needed. Cassidy grabbed Aldan's hand and twisted his arm behind his back.

The maneuver was awkward. Aldan had a foot on her height and almost twice as much muscle mass over her. She was forced to look around him as looking over his shoulder wasn't an option.

"Convincing," he grunted, trying to wiggle his arm loose to provide some relief, but Cassidy's grip on his arm didn't allow it.

Resting the blaster against his head she marched them forward. All eyes followed them, and she could feel the squadron's attention centre on her hand that now held both the weapon and the detonator.

"They're going to shoot us. You know that, right?"

"The thought had crossed my mind."

"And?"

"And I'm open to suggestions."

Aldan remained quiet, his silence pensive.

"Okay, let's run through it," Cassidy said in her best lecturer's voice. "If we leave the dome, they shoot us because they're no longer at risk of getting blown up."

"And we still are."

"Precisely."

"All right. So, we'll need a method of escape once we're out there."

"Any suggestions on how to accomplish that?"

"Definitely not."

"Great." Cassidy eyed the approaching barrier.

"Stalling won't work." When Cassidy didn't answer, Aldan continued. "They'll call our bluff about detonating and capture us."

Cassidy hummed in agreement. She wracked her brain trying to think of an alternative plan.

A commotion behind them interrupted her train of thought. There was the sound of yelling, and Cassidy turned to witness a scuffle where Nyler had joined their ranks.

Aldan stopped short. "What the—"

An engine revved. The sound seemed thunderous in the tense silence that surrounded the stalemate. Soldiers scrambled to break formation as an armoured vehicle lurched into the square and slammed on the acceleration.

The sound of blaster fire rang out and the pair ducked.

"Hold your fire!" the commander screamed. "You'll blow the dome!"

The vehicle barrelled toward Cassidy and Aldan without showing signs of slowing. Cassidy had readied herself to launch out of the way when Aldan wrapped an arm around her waist. "Wrong way."

"What!"

"Hold on!"

Before she could protest, he stepped into the path of the oncoming vehicle. Cassidy unceremoniously jammed the detonation device into her pocket—the silly thing hadn't been activated to begin with—and squeezed her eyes shut.

The armoured truck swerved, and Aldan grabbed one of the railings that wrapped around the side of it. Grunting, he swung them up into the bed of the truck.

"Glad you could make it," Nyler quipped through the back opening of the cab from where he sat in the driver's seat.

"Took you long enough," Aldan shot back.

Nyler grinned in response and slammed the driving gear to its fastest setting. They sped toward the barrier. "I wanted to give you time to come up with a plan."

"You should've taken longer, then." Aldan looked down and realized his arm was still around Cassidy's waist. His face reddened around the mask he wore. He opened his mouth to say something, then jerked his head back toward the square. "Duck!"

Cassidy dropped to her knees as a beam of light shot past them in a wide arc. The ground rumbled where it made contact.

"That wasn't even close," Nyler shouted back at them. "It's like they were trying to miss."

"They are." Cassidy shaded her eyes with a hand and assessed the soldiers behind them.

Aldan's expression was one of grim agreement. "They're herding us."

"To where?"

"To where they can detonate us safely."

Cassidy heard Nyler's sharp intake of breath. "Why?" The question was desperate.

Aldan's gaze flicked to where the transfer device was hidden in his inside pocket.

"Because they never had any intention of letting us escape." Cassidy frowned. "They've been waiting for the best moment to get rid of us with the least amount of damage."

Nyler's driving didn't falter. "So what do we do?"

Cassidy pursed her lips. She slid her gaze from the pocket inside Aldan's open coat, to the explosive device that was still wrapped around his chest. She looked at the one strapped around her own torso, then raised her eyes to Aldan's. "We give them what they want."

"What?"

"They want an explosion? Let's give them one." Cassidy banged her hand on the top of the driver's cab. "Slow down, Nyler."

Nyler looked at her with surprise but did as he was told.

Aldan looked thoughtful as Cassidy climbed between them, unclasping their explosive devices and holding them by the straps. She waited until they approached the barrier.

"I hope you didn't get kicked out of the military for being a lousy shot," she said to Aldan as she began to swing one of the devices in a circular motion, using the strap as a sling.

Aldan ripped his mask off and grinned, sliding his blaster from his belt holster just as Cassidy lobbed the first brick of clay into the air. She waited several heartbeats before releasing the next one, and then the next, timing it so that they synced into the same, spaced-out, downward arch.

Aldan cocked his weapon. "Go," he told Nyler, who slammed the vehicle into top speed.

He fired one shot and the device closest to them exploded. The resulting force bridged the gap and set off the other explosives, rocking the area around them.

Cassidy was thrown backward from the force. She slammed into the cab of the vehicle and grabbed the side to keep from falling off. Next to her Aldan did the same. The back tires lifted off the road before smashing back down with an impact that jarred her bones.

Surprise and horror sent a chill down her spine as they sped through the exit and away from the dome.

The explosions had caught the dome's slanted ceiling. The inside shield wasn't as strong as the outside by design. The outside rock was fortified against the atmospheric chemicals, and a huge section had blown outward from the force, creating a gaping hole that now acted as a vacuum.

The soldiers were too preoccupied to follow them as the trio sped into the wasteland. Alarm bells rang and lights flashed. Cassidy stared wide-eyed at the commotion behind them as the mobilized forces fell back to safer ground. She could see them moving their equipment to erect a barricade under the crumbling rock.

Next to her, Aldan lowered his blaster in surprise. "Oops."

CHAPTER FOURTEEN

Cassidy kept her gaze focused on the approaching mountain range ahead of them.

Aldan holstered his blaster and stood next to her. "No one got hurt, Cassidy." His voice was gentle as he answered her unasked question.

Cassidy couldn't meet his eye. "How do you know?"

Aldan shrugged a shoulder. "The military provides blast-resistance uniforms. And the block had already been evacuated—there were no civilians to injure."

Cassidy eyed his coat and remembered how it had snapped into a shield to protect them. She frowned. "But the atmosphere—"

"—Is inconsequential." Aldan gave her a lopsided grin. "The domes can fail at any moment. Every building has masks and an evaluation plan in place for that possibility."

Cassidy felt the tension from her shoulders disappear. There was no reason for him to lie. He'd been nothing but honest with her up until this point.

Aldan took a step closer, and Cassidy found herself looking up into his yellow eyes. "You have a fierce and beautiful heart, Cassidy Cane."

Cassidy felt her cheeks heat at his words.

"We've got company," Nyler warned. His voice was muffled by the breathing mask he slapped on when they exited the dome.

Aldan and Cassidy turned. One of the army vehicles had broken away from the barricade to pursue them through the wasteland.

Aldan swore.

A shadow fell across them as Nyler entered the mountain range.

"Pull in over there," Aldan told Nyler, pointing to a large hollow ahead in the distance. "We'll have to double back to throw them off our trail."

"We?"

"Aren't you coming with us?" Aldan cocked his head at Nyler. "Unless you'd rather wait here for the soldiers to arrive…"

Nyler grinned. "I thought you'd never ask." He expertly maneuvered the stolen vehicle under the rocky overhang before killing the engine. The three of them hopped down and began to pile loose stones and boulders along the side to partially cover it.

Cassidy surveyed their handiwork. It looked like a botched hiding attempt. Their pursuers would be drawn to it immediately. It was perfect. "Let's go."

Aldan led the way to the cave where he and Cassidy had appeared earlier that day.

Nyler gave them an incredulous look when they entered. "What are you doing?"

Cassidy fought the urge to grin. She couldn't blame

his hesitation. It looked as though they were dragging him into an underground tunnel.

Well, they were. But this one had a hidden exit.

She stepped into the tunnel, motioning for Nyler to follow her. Her arms were outstretched as she walked, using them to feel the edges of the tunnel as they hurried through it and into the cave at the end. Almost immediately, she could feel the familiar prickle of a nearby portal on her right. Moving closer, she plunged her hand into it without hesitation, feeling the shock of cold that reverberated down her arm just as Aldan illuminated it with his gloves.

Nyler's jaw dropped when he saw her arm disappear into the solid rock wall. "How...?"

Cassidy didn't answer. Instead, she pulled her arm back out. She kept her left hand against the cave wall and took a few steps forward. There, ahead in the distance, she could feel the faint pull of a second portal.

It was the portal home.

"It's a secret." Aldan's tone was light, but his expression said it all—it was a secret to be protected. He stepped toward her and motioned for Cassidy to turn around, rummaging in the pack she still wore to pull out several force shield projectors.

He took a moment to assess where to place them, finally choosing spots where, once the wall was formed, it would offer no view of the cave past the tunnel.

"I can't block the whole tunnel. They would notice that. But this cave should suffice." Aldan brought the projectors online with a few taps of his glove.

With a start, Cassidy realized that, unlike on Telluria,

Aldan wasn't creating a barrier to the cave, he was going to fill in the entire cave. He wasn't taking any chances of the Alluvians breaking through an unmonitored rock wall and finding the way to Telluria.

"I hope your device works quickly," Nyler frowned.

Aldan winced in agreement. "The visual projection powers up first, then the force shield. So long as they don't stick their arms in it..." He walked around the cave, attaching more of the projectors to the walls as he did. With a single tap against his glove, he activated them. "That should do it."

The two men looked expectantly at Cassidy.

"Is it safe?" she asked.

Aldan gave a gentle smile, knowing what she meant. "Our reinforcements would have arrived long before now to cause a distraction. If there had been a problem, the Tellurian government would have come through the portal as soon as they discovered it.

Cassidy nodded. That made sense. There was no danger in them returning to Telluria.

Aldan inclined his head. "Shall we?"

"No."

The word came out more hollow than she intended.

Nyler's eyes widened, but Cassidy barely noticed as her attention was mostly focused on Aldan. His stare burned into her as she took a step sideways—not forward—around the Tellurian portal.

She could feel the pull of the second portal. The one that she had missed the last time she returned from Alluvia. The one that led to Earth. "I have to go home."

The only sound was the rock wall building itself along

the parameters Aldan had programmed. He stepped forward and extended a hand. Not for her, she realized, but for the pack she still wore across her back. Aldan flipped it open then, to her surprise, simply closed it again and returned it to her. She slung it slowly over one shoulder.

"Cassidy..." Aldan's expression was unreadable. There was a beat of silence, then he and Nyler snapped to attention—their keen sense of hearing picking up what Cassidy's could not. "Go."

"They're coming," Nyler declared at the same instant. In his haste, he stepped backwards into the tunnel that led to Telluria. Caddisy could see his expression of surprise before he disappeared completely into the rock face.

Aldan's eyes flicked to the wall that was slowly building itself into the empty space of the tunnel, then back to her as she stood there, halfway between the two portals.

Their eyes met for the briefest of moments. "*Go*," he said again, his voice soft.

She could hear the approaching soldiers. The wall projection blocked them from view, but Cassidy knew that the shield was not yet fully functional, and she fervently hoped that they wouldn't think to inspect the back wall of the tunnel.

Aldan grasped Cassidy's arms and turned her so that she was facing him. He gave her a smile, a smile that lit up his yellow eyes and caused her fingertips to tingle, then pushed her backward without warning.

He watched her as she fell, his expression unreadable.

He gave her one last look, then pivoted and threw himself after Nyler as the cave closed in on itself. He disappeared as Alluvia faded from sight, and the view of the planet became obstructed by a solid rock wall that had appeared from thin air.

***

Cassidy slammed into the ground, catching herself with her elbow to lessen the impact. She lay there for several minutes, breathing, as she waited and reoriented herself.

She was alone.

The air was unmistakably familiar. She took gasping breaths, feeling relief as the noxious vapors from Alluvia were expelled from her lungs and replaced with the sweet-smelling air from her home planet.

She was back on Earth.

Cassidy groaned and sat up, carefully sliding Aldan's pack to the ground. Opening the top flap, she spied the object that Aldan had placed in there—a folded over piece of fabric. She pulled it open and was surprised to see alien, hand-written lettering had been burned into it—undoubtedly another function of the multi-purpose gloves that he wore. She held it up to get a better look.

> *Use these crumbs to find your way back.*
> > *Your Hansel,*
> > *Aldan.*

Cassidy peered inside the pack and was amazed at the Tellurian technology that Aldan had allowed her to bring back to Earth. She tucked the note into her coat pocket and secured the pack. Gamgee would be delighted to get his hands on these inventions, but there was no real scientific reason for her to turn over the note. Besides, he would probably hear all about it soon enough.

Cassidy rose and dusted off her pants, turning in the direction where she had left her car all those days ago.

A large grin spread across her face as she began to make her way home. Cassidy had a feeling that this wouldn't be the last of the Tellurian Terrorist.

EPILOGUE

Tallis stood alone in the park, squeezing his stress ball in his hand. He was standing beside the see-saw where there were children playing, but he was not with them nor was he watching them.

In the far distance, far enough away that they wouldn't have noticed him staring even if they'd looked in his direction, a family of four walked together along the foot path.

It was Preston and Kayla Cane and two of their three children, Margo and Rica. They walked and laughed and ate ice cream and talked about something pleasant he couldn't make out.

As he watched them, he started to squeeze the stress ball harder, and faster.

ACKNOWLEDGEMENTS

The authors would like to pay special thanks to the *Slipstreamers* committee at Engen Books, including Amanda Labonté, Matthew LeDrew, Ali House, Ellen Curtis, and, Erin Vance.

Without their tireless efforts, none of this would have been possible.

Special thanks to this episode's editor, AJ Ryan.

Lauralana Dunne would also like to thank the rest of the Slipstreamer Committee who helped to bring everything together, as well as all of the authors who signed onto the project: their open minds and collaborative spirit helped to make the series the success that it is. Above all, heartfelt thanks and appreciation is extended to AJ Ryan and JD Ryot, as without their hard work none of this would have been possible.

ABOUT THE AUTHOR

Lauralana Dunne grew up running around the library stacks of St. John's, Newfoundland, Canada, and has been writing stories for as long as she can remember. She can often be found at different writing events around the city, typing on her phone with one hand while simultaneously fueling her caffeine addiction with the other.

She is a die-hard lover of YA Fantasy, and has been known to describe herself as a "Slayer of Imaginary Monsters."

Het first novel, *Ashes*, was published in 2020.

JD Ryot is the reclusive creator of the *Slipstreamers* series from Engen Books. JD is an avid fan of young adult literature and adventure serials. When asked if they had come to this world through a portal themselves, JD Ryot refused to answer. No record of their birth has ever been found... on this world.